Julius Lester

Harcourt, Inc. • Orlando   Austin   New York   San Diego   Toronto   London

A
Tale
of Love
and Desire

www.HarcourtBooks.com

Library of Congress Cataloging-in-Publication Data
Lester, Julius.
Cupid: a tale of love and desire/Julius Lester.
p.   cm.
Summary: A retelling of the classic tale in which Cupid, the god of love, falls in love with the beautiful mortal, Psyche.
[1. Cupid (Roman deity)—Fiction.   2. Psyche (Greek deity)—Fiction.   3. Mythology, Classical—Fiction.   4. Love—Fiction.]   I. Title.
PZ7.L5629Cup   2007
[Fic]—dc22   2006001946
ISBN-13: 978-0-15-202056-9   ISBN-10: 0-15-202056-X

Text set in Minion
Designed by Lauren Rille

First edition

H G F E D C B A

Printed in the United States of America

For Milan,

who daily shows me the beauty of love

Introducing Psyche

A long time ago, when Time was still winding its watch and Sun was trying to figure out which way was east and which was west, there was a king and queen. I don't know what country they were king and queen of. That information was not in the story when it came down to me. Sometimes, stories don't understand; what may not be important to them is very important to us.

Now, I'm sure there are people who can tell this particular story without having a name for the kingdom this king and queen ruled. Jupiter bless them. I guess I'm not that good of a storyteller, because I need a name for the kingdom. I asked the story if it would mind my giving the place a name. It didn't see any harm in it, so I am going to call it the Kingdom-by-the-Great-Blue-Sea.

The story also does not have names for the king and queen. I know they had names, but nobody would say to them, "What's up, Chuck?" or say, "Looky here, Liz," if those happened to be their names. I am in agreement with the story this time. If nobody could use their names, there is no need to have them in the story. As for what the king and queen called each other, they were probably like any other married couple and he called her "Honey" and "Sweetheart," and she called him "Good Lips" and things like that, which we don't need to pursue any further.

The king and queen had three daughters. I know what you are thinking: the daughters didn't have names, either. That is partly true. Two of the girls were name-naked. I'm not even into the story yet and already we have four people that the Internal Revenue Service could not send a letter to.

Well, the daughters need names. The story is content to call them the "elder sister" and the "younger sister." That is not good enough for me. The two sisters have to have names. I was thinking about having a contest to pick their names, but the story would probably get tired of waiting for all the votes to be counted, catch a bus, and go to somebody else to get told and that person would not tell the story the way it should be told, which is how I am going to tell it. So, I'll name them myself. I'll call one Thomasina, after a girl I had a lot of lust for in high school who wasn't lusting after me (bet she's sorry now), and I'll call the other one Calla. I have no idea if there is such a name, but it sounds like it belongs in the story.

Thomasina and Calla were the two older girls and they were very beautiful. Both had long, pale yellow hair that came down to their waists. They would get up early every morning and sit in chairs on the balcony outside their room, and two serving girls would brush the morning sunlight into their hair. They would have been the most beautiful young women in the land if not for someone else—their younger sister.

Her name was Psyche, which is pronounced *sigh-key*, and it means "soul." It also means "butterfly." Maybe that's what the soul is like—fragile, colorful, and beautiful like a butterfly, and maybe Psyche was so beautiful because people could see her soul in her face.

I tried to write something that would give you an idea of how beautiful she was, but the letters of the alphabet got so confused and jumbled up trying to arrange themselves into words to describe someone for whom there were no words, they ended up crying in frustration. I hate trying to make words out of letters that have been crying and are so wet they can't stay on the page. Later on in the story, after the letters dry off, I'll try again to arrange them into enough words so you'll have some idea of what Psyche looked like. For now, you'll just have to believe me when I say she was the most beautiful woman in the world.

The people of the kingdom said Psyche had to be a goddess because she was even more beautiful than Venus, the goddess of love, who until now had been the most beautiful woman in creation.

The news of Psyche's beauty spread all over the world. Soon, people came to see Psyche from everywhere—Rome, Rumania; Lagos, Latvia; Moscow, Mississippi; Green Bay, Ghana; Paris, Poland; and Zurich, Zimbabwe.

3

Every day around the time people's shadows snuck beneath their feet to get out of the sun, the tall wooden doors to the palace grounds swung open, and Psyche came out to take her daily walk. Men, women, children, and all the creatures stopped what they were doing to look at her. Birds flying by would see Psyche, stop flapping their wings, and fall to the ground. Ants would be toting crumbs which, to them, were as big as China. They could not see anything of Psyche except a sixteenth of an inch of her big toenail, but that was enough for them to be so overcome by her beauty that they dropped their crumbs and just stared.

Psyche walked along the road that led from the palace to the outskirts of the largest village, which wasn't far, and then she walked back and the palace doors would close behind her. But, for the rest of the day, not much got done in the kingdom because everybody and every creature was thinking about Psyche. Cows didn't make milk; sheep didn't grow wool; hens forgot to lay eggs. The butcher didn't slaughter animals; the baker's bread and cakes burned in the oven; and the candlestick-maker was in too much of a daze to dip his wicks in tallow.

Well, this was not good for the economy. The economy went into a recession, then a depression, and finally, went into a cul-de-sac, which is different from a paper sack and a gunnysack and a sad sack as well as a sack on the quarterback.

The king had to do something or the economy was going to collapse. He thought the matter over and decided that if Psyche went for a walk only one afternoon each month, the economy would be all right.

"I don't appreciate your deciding what I can do and when I can do it," Psyche told her father.

"The economy is more important than your happiness," the king replied.

That tells you right there what kind of king he was! Who in his right mind would make the economy more important than a person's well-being? But he was the king, and what he said was the way things had to be.

He must have been asleep the day in kinging school when the teacher talked about the law of supply and demand. When the supply of something diminishes and the demand for it goes up, it is going to cost more. The king was about to pay a very high price, because the demand to see Psyche was about to destroy the kingdom.

The birds and the insects carried word of the king's decree to the farthest ends of the four directions, which happened to be ten thousand miles on the other side of next week. Everybody and everything went into a panic because nobody knew anymore what day or time Psyche would take her walk. There was only one way anybody could be sure of seeing her. People in other kingdoms started calling in sick to work. I know they didn't have telephones back in those days. When I say they called in sick, I mean they stuck their heads out the door of their houses and yelled, "I got the flu in my eyetooth and can't come to work!" Then they moved to the Kingdom-by-the-Great-Blue-Sea so they could be there whenever Psyche took her walk.

Before long the kingdom was overrun with all kinds of people who did not speak the language, did not know the customs, and, furthermore, did not care. All they wanted was to see Psyche. So many people moved to the kingdom, a lot of stress was put on the infrastructure, which is another way of saying that there weren't enough bathrooms and toilet paper for everybody. The king solved that problem in a hurry, though exactly how is not in the story. But I can tell you this much: Shondie the shovel-maker and Tyrone the toilet-paper-maker became very wealthy men in a short period of time.

But, even after the infrastructure got its infra restructured, the king and queen still had a problem. And that was Psyche.

Psyche's Beauty

Besides being so beautiful, Psyche was also very intelligent, unlike her sisters who thought about nothing except what clothes to put on. Psyche, however, thought about the important things, like Who am I? and What is the meaning of my life? Every morning when she looked in the mirror, she wondered: "What is beauty? What do others see that makes them think I am beautiful?"

She would stare at her image in the mirror and try to see herself as others did. Unlike her sisters, Psyche's hair was dark and gleaming because each night before going to bed she stood on the balcony outside her room and brushed nightshine into her hair until it was radiant with blackness. Sun was as entranced by her beauty as were people, and when she came outside, if only to walk in the palace garden, he stroked her skin with his softest light until she was the color of sand.

Looking at herself in the mirror, she wondered: "Does my beauty reside in my heart-shaped face, large eyes, and full lips? What makes one person a joy to look at while another is not, and still another's face leaves people's hearts neither gladdened nor repulsed?"

Eventually, she would sigh and move away from the mirror, her questions unanswered. She did not understand what beauty was, but she knew this: being beautiful made her lonely. Noblemen came to the palace and courted Thomasina and Calla, and before long, both were married and moved away to nearby kingdoms.

But no young men came for Psyche. When the king had banquets in the Great Hall of the palace, he would seat Psyche between single men of the best families, but in the presence of her beauty, the young men's tongues were as heavy as mountains. Yet, with the other young women present at those banquets, words flowed from those same tongues like melodies from the throats of birds in the spring.

One day Psyche asked her parents, "What is it that makes me beautiful? And what is beauty?"

They were not sure how to answer either the question or the look of concern on their daughter's face, nor the anguish in her voice.

The king laughed nervously. "Those are questions for my philosopher. I'll send him to you tomorrow. He will tell you more about beauty than you want to know."

"No, Father. I'm asking you and Mother."

It was now the queen's turn to give a nervous laugh. "Don't concern yourself with questions that have no answers. Be glad you are not ugly."

The king saw tears come into Psyche's eyes and realized that he and the queen were not taking Psyche seriously enough.

"Is it that you want to know what others see when they look at you?" he asked quietly.

Psyche nodded, grateful that perhaps he understood.

The king thought for a long while, then said, "There was an orchid that used to grow in the mountains. It was very rare and its beauty was unlike that of any flower ever seen. My grandfather took me to the copse where it grew, because this orchid was found no other place in the world. I could not have been more than seven years old, yet I still remember it as if it were only this morning. A few months after he showed me the orchid, the gods sent terrible storms off the Great Blue Sea. The salt water from the sea blew far inland and destroyed many trees and plants. The following spring, my grandfather and I returned to the copse where the orchid grew. Alas, the storm had filled the ground with salt and the orchid could not grow. However, each spring I go back to that place and look for it. It is gone, but the memory of the orchid's beauty has stayed with me all these years. I cannot tell you what it was about the orchid that made it so beautiful. It may have been its colors, its shape. Or it may have been the combination of the two, which created something more than the two did separately. I can only tell you that seeing the orchid made me feel wonderful, made me feel that my life, even at age seven, was greater than everything I knew and everything I would know. The memory of that orchid continues to expand my life beyond the limitations of my body and my mind." He smiled. "So it is with your beauty, my darling girl. It is a gift to all those who have the privilege of seeing it. People look at you and they feel better."

But Psyche was not so easily mollified. "I suppose it's nice that my beauty is a gift to others, but that does not answer my question. What is that beauty to me? *That* is what I want to know."

"You are an ungrateful child!" her mother rebuked her. "Every female in the kingdom would do anything to have your beauty."

"There are days I wish I could give it to them," Psyche responded sadly. "Let one of them live with this loneliness."

And the king and queen and their youngest daughter lapsed into an uncomfortable silence.

Venus

All the gods and goddesses lived on Olympus, which was pretty much like Earth. It had mountains, valleys, streams, forests, but no deserts. The major difference was that Earth existed under the sky. Olympus was behind the sky. I'm not exactly sure where that is, but I know it's north of here but south of there.

I would take you on a tour and show you all the different palaces where the gods and goddesses lived, but the story says we don't have time for that. One of the hard things about being a storyteller is that stories can be impatient. When it's their time to be told, they get real mean if they think you're taking too long with the telling. So we had better hurry to the outskirts of Olympus to the palace of Venus, the goddess of love.

Venus lived away from the other deities because she didn't want them knowing all of her business. Even though she was married to Vulcan, the god of metalwork, she did not have much talent for monogamy. How could she? She was the goddess of love, and love was what she was faithful to. If her husband did not understand that, he should not have married her. Of course, I can hear you saying that if Venus knew that about herself, she should have stayed single. I would try and explain it to you, but the story just told me I was about to get off on a tangent, and it does not have time for that. I agree. The surest way to get a headache is trying to understand the doings of the gods and god-desses. So let's move on, because I don't need a headache.

Venus's palace was made from the soft, rosy colors of sunset and the glowing ivory white of moonlight. It was large because it had to accommodate all the spirits that came there. The first floor was reserved for Venus and her son, Cupid. They lived in their own wings, at opposite ends of the palace. The second floor was set aside for the spirits of people whose hearts had been broken in love; the third floor was for the spirits of those who had not loved wisely. (My spirit was there more than once to recuperate from letting my eyes take my heart where it did not belong.) The fourth floor was the most crowded. It was for the spirits of the lonely.

Venus did not have much to do except make regular visits to her temples on Earth. (A temple was like a church, except there was no organ or gospel choir.) People would bring her offerings and she would listen to their love problems. How much and how closely Venus listened depended on what you brought her, and Venus did not like anything cheap. But caviar, champagne, or anything made of cashmere always got you her undivided attention.

However, of late, Venus had not seen any caviar, champagne, or cashmere. People had stopped coming to her temples, and she did not know why. On this particular afternoon, the goddess was going to learn the reason.

She was lying on a chaise lounge on the front porch of her palace, getting a massage. Every week Venus set aside six days to be pampered. She would get a massage from Oizys, the goddess of pain, then sit in the hot tub and drink champagne and eat strawberries. After that she would get her nails and hair done. Then her fashion stylist would bring in a rack of the latest gowns from Oscar de la Olympus, and Venus would try on each one. Being pampered was exhausting, so she would take a nap and wake up in time for dinner, which that evening was going to be steak Diane sautéed in ambrosia and grapes, with rice and peas smothered with nectar. On the seventh day of every week, Venus rested from being pampered and went to her temples to receive gifts and the adulation of the people. At least that was how it used to be.

On this particular day, Venus had started to doze off beneath the skillful hands of Oizys, when the goddess of pain said, under her breath, "I wonder what's going on down there."

Of all the deities, Oizys was the most ignored. There were no temples dedicated to her honor. There weren't even any stories about her like there were about Jupiter, Juno, Apollo, and Venus, among others. But because the deities avoided Oizys, except when they wanted a hard massage, she had plenty of time to see who was doing what to whom and why. She knew more about the doings on Olympus than any of them, including Mercury, who did nothing but carry messages and gossip all over everywhere. So when Oizys said, as if speaking to herself, "I wonder what's going on down there," she knew what was going on down there. She also knew the information would cause Venus great pain. But if it were not for pain, neither deities nor mortals would ever grow up.

"What's going on where?" Venus asked sleepily. "Ouch! Not so hard on my shoulders. Ahh! Yes, that's better." She sighed and closed her eyes. "Did you say something was going on?" she asked sleepily.

"Over there," Oizys replied, pointing to a tiny kingdom at the edge of the Great Blue Sea. "All those people. They look like they're waiting for something, or someone."

Reluctantly, Venus raised up and looked down on the world. It took her a moment to find what Oizys was pointing to, but finally she saw crowds lining both sides of a road. Venus smiled wistfully. "That's how it used to be when I walked among mortals," she thought.

The crowd stirred as the great doors to the palace grounds swung open. People jostled each other to get a better view.

"The king of this realm must be very loved," Venus whispered. She was eager to see the man who inspired such devotion from his subjects.

But the person who walked out was a young woman of a beauty unlike any Venus had ever seen, including that which looked back at her from her mirror each morning. The crowds were so quiet you could hear green color flowing into new leaves. Some people were so overcome at the sight of the young woman, they fainted. Others simply gazed, tears streaming down their faces.

As the young woman continued walking, petals from flowers bordering the road drifted off the blooms, braided themselves into a wreath, and settled on her head.

"Who is that?" Venus demanded to know, not wanting to believe what she was seeing.

"Oh, I wonder if that is who I overheard Mars and Apollo talking about the other day." Oizys stopped suddenly, as if afraid that she had said too much. Not too long ago, Mars and Venus had a passionate affair. When Vulcan learned of it, he rigged a net over her bed. The next time she and Mars lay together, the net fell on them. Vulcan had called all the gods and goddesses to come and look at the two in their naked togetherness.

Venus frowned at the mention of her former lover's name. Even though they were no longer lovers, she did not like the idea of him looking at another woman, especially a mortal.

"What were Mars and Apollo saying?"

"Oh, nothing," Oizys muttered.

"Answer me!"

"It was nothing. Just men talking, and you know how they are. What they said is not worth repeating."

"I'll determine what is and is not worth repeating. Now, tell me what was said."

Oizys sighed again, but smiled to herself. She had set a trap for Venus even more subtly than Vulcan had. "Well, they said she was more beautiful than any goddess on Olympus."

Venus was furious. "Who said that?" she demanded to know. "Which one of them?"

"It was Apollo," said Oizys, feigning reluctance.

"Apollo!" Venus exclaimed. It would have broken her heart had Mars spoken the words, but it was worse coming from Apollo because he was incapable of telling a lie.

But Oizys was not, for it was she who had just put a lie into Apollo's mouth.

"Who do *you* think is the most beautiful woman in all of creation?" Venus asked.

"You are," Oizys responded hastily. "What mortal could come close to matching your great beauty?"

What mortal, indeed? Venus said silently. "What is the name of this—this thing on Earth who thinks she is more beautiful than I?"

"I believe Apollo referred to her as Psyche."

"Psyche!" Venus repeated in disgust. "Leave me, Oizys."

"But, goddess, I have not finished your massage. Nothing would be more soothing at such a moment than a deep massage."

"Yes, yes, I know, but I need to be alone. Now, leave me."

Smiling to herself, Oizys picked up her vials of oils and left.

Venus went inside where the hot tub had already been filled with steaming water by her servants. She disrobed, stepped in, and sat down. She had to do something about this Psyche. Could she be the reason people had stopped coming to worship Venus at her temples? Perhaps people had forgotten just how beautiful she was. She would go immediately to her temple in the Kingdom-by-the-Great-Blue-Sea. When people saw her, they would remember what true beauty looked like, and they would abandon their foolish adulation of that young woman whose beauty was merely mortal and would fade sooner than later.

When Venus finished her bath, her servants, the Three Graces—Aglaia, Charis, and Pasithea—came quickly with towels made from the warm breezes of South Wind. They dried her, then dressed her in a white gown of silk and cashmere. The goddess's long, dark straight hair was oiled until each strand shone with the luster of desire. By then, her golden chariot drawn by swans was waiting for her on the great lawn outside her palace. The Graces helped Venus into the chariot, then she flew down to reclaim her rightful place in the hearts of the people.

When she arrived at her temple on a hillside by the Great Blue Sea, Venus was shocked at what she saw. The temple's roof was sagging; the altar on which supplicants used to place offerings had fallen over and was covered with dust and spiderwebs. The marble floor could barely be seen beneath thick layers of dead leaves. Where were the temple's caretakers? Were they, too, among the crowds waiting for the appearance of Psyche?

Angry, Venus returned to her swan-drawn chariot and

flew to the very road Psyche had walked along mere hours before. People still lingered there, hoping the young woman would come out again. No one noticed Venus's chariot when it landed in front of the huge doors to the palace. No one noticed when the goddess began walking along the road. Venus looked into the faces of the people, hoping to see a spark of recognition in their eyes. But although their eyes were open, they could not see Venus for looking at the image of Psyche imprinted on their minds.

Unable to abide the humiliation an instant longer, Venus returned quickly to Olympus, more furious than she had ever been. If she didn't do something, she was going to find herself wandering through the world and being ignored. That's what happened to gods and goddesses when people stopped believing in them. She had seen them— Astarte, Isis, Osiris, Marduk, Gilgamesh—so many of the old deities walking among the people who did not recognize them. It was as if they had never existed, but deities could not die. If no one recognized your existence, however, was that not death?

"Where in Jupiter's name is Cupid?" she screamed.

If ever she needed her son, it was now. He knew better than anyone how to torture humans with lust and love. Indeed, she herself knew just how powerful the love potion was that Cupid put on his arrows. She still grieved for a love unlike any she had ever known or would ever know again.

Venus and Adonis

It happened when Cupid was still a child. Venus was visiting her temples, but her mind was not focused on the love problems of mortals. She was thinking about Cupid, whom she missed more than she thought possible. She finished her temple duties quickly and hurried back to Olympus and her beloved son.

"I'm going to get you," she announced playfully, standing in the doorway of his chambers.

Cupid knew that meant she was going to tickle him, and he began giggling. He was sitting on his bed and hurriedly crawled beneath the blanket as his mother came toward him.

But just as Venus reached the bed, she tripped over Cupid's bow, which was lying on the floor. She fell onto the bed—and the quiver of arrows Cupid had carelessly tossed there when he had come in from practicing.

His mother had told him countless times, "Cupid! Hang your bow and quiver on the back of the closet door." But, yet once again, he had forgotten, or more likely, not felt like doing as his mother asked.

A gold-tipped arrow was sticking out of the quiver, and the tip penetrated the skin just above Venus's breasts. She gasped. Both she and Cupid knew what had happened. He laughed! Venus wanted to slap him, but the arrow's potion would make her fall hopelessly in love with the first person she saw. Juno forbid that should be her own son! Shielding her eyes, she ran from the room, down the long corridor, across the entranceway, and into her suite, in the opposite wing, the sound of Cupid's laughter in her ears.

For three days Venus kept to her chambers and saw no one. The wound appeared to heal quickly, but the potion on the arrowhead was more potent than she knew. Some of the potion was still in her bloodstream.

Thinking herself healed, Venus went outside and looked down on Earth to see what had transpired in the days she had locked herself away. The first person she saw was a young man of amazing beauty and faster than the blink of her eyes, she wanted him, needed him, could not conceive of being able to live without him. Too late she realized: she was still infected, but she did not care. Never in the years of her eternity had she loved anyone as she loved the one on whom she was gazing at that moment.

His name was Adonis, and he was as handsome as Venus was beautiful. He was standing in a meadow, practicing throwing his spear, when out of the sky came a golden chariot drawn by two swans. Even before Venus took one step toward him, he only needed the slightest of glances to be as in love with her as she was with him. What mortal could have resisted the goddess of love?

Venus had loved many, but her feelings for all the others had as much substance as fog compared to her ardor for Adonis. In the past, she realized, she had confused love with lust. But lust was nothing except caring for one's own pleasure. As long as her lust was sated, it had not mattered to her whom she lay with. However, with Adonis, lust was replaced by a deep and passionate caring for the well-being and happiness of another.

Adonis loved to hunt, and Venus gladly went with him, running alongside her lover through woods and over hills, as he chased after rabbit and deer.

However, Adonis became bored hunting harmless game. Where was the challenge in that? He wanted to go after bigger and more dangerous animals, like boars, wolves, bears, and lions, animals whose teeth were bloody after they had killed and eaten. But Venus was afraid for him.

"My love. The time for boldness is when you hunt the animals that are timid and run away at the sound of your footsteps. Do not go after the beasts who do not quail before human boldness. What are your two arms and legs compared to the four limbs and many teeth of the beasts? I beg you. Do not be bold when to do so is to put my heart at risk. Do not place your desire to prove yourself above my love. Your beauty enchants me, but it does not move the hearts of the boar, wolf, bear, or lion."

Reluctantly, Adonis respected her wishes. But the day came when Venus had to attend to her duties as goddess, duties she had neglected so she could be with Adonis.

As soon as Venus and her swan-drawn chariot flew heavenward, Adonis went into the woods. How odd, but almost immediately a boar stood in the path as if waiting for him and him alone. Some say this was no ordinary boar, but Mars in the guise of the tusked beast because he was jealous that Venus loved someone more than she had loved him. Others maintain that the boar was Vulcan, angry, yet again, that Venus was making a mockery of their marriage.

But perhaps the boar was only a boar. Adonis, eager to test himself and his skill, threw his spear at the animal. Alas. The tip of the weapon penetrated only far enough into the boar's tough hide to anger but not wound it. With its long tusks, the animal dislodged the spear. Angry now, the boar charged Adonis.

What are the two legs of a man to the four of a beast? The boar easily caught him. Adonis screamed as the tusks went deeply into his side and chest.

Venus was scarcely halfway on her journey to her temple on Atlantis when she heard a loud and terrified cry in the voice she knew from all others on Earth and Olympus.

"Adonis!" Quickly, she turned the chariot around. Even from afar she could see her beloved's body lying on the forest path, wrapped in blood as if it were a cloak. The swans had scarcely set the chariot on the ground before Venus was running to him. He was already dead.

Holding him on her lap, she cried out to the Fates, "How could you allow this to happen? But I will not let you have all the victory!"

She sprinkled nectar on Adonis's voluptuously red, red blood. The blood began to bubble. Then arising from it came a blood-colored flower as light and delicate as slowly healing sorrow. This is how the anemone, also known as the wind flower, came into being. It is a flower whose petals are weak, and when a wind blows against them, they fall and die.

It was a sad but fitting memorial to the beautiful Adonis.

Even now Venus could not think of Adonis without his loss throbbing within her as if it had its own heart. He had been taken from her, and now this Psyche was taking the love of the people from her. There was nothing she could have done to prevent Adonis's death, but she would make Psyche wish she had never been born.

Enter Cupid

When you think of Cupid, I bet you see a cute, chubby baby with little wings and a bow and arrow. As many times as I've been in lust *and* in love (and if the truth be told, I was in lust a lot more than I was in love), I know that a diaper-wearing baby had nothing to do with it. It took a god with a devious mind and no morals to get me entangled with some of the women to whom I proclaimed eternal love.

So if you are thinking that you're going to hear a story about some rosy-cheeked little boy flying around in the clouds, you should close the book now. The Cupid I'm going to tell you about was a young man who was tall and very handsome. His body was so sculpted, you could see every muscle, sinew, and tendon. Long, flowing wings grew out of his shoulder blades like a melody looking for a singer.

Of all the deities, he was probably the most beautiful, which befits the god of love. His special emblem was the rose, and as you know, a rose is beautiful to look at and beautiful to smell, but its stem is studded with thorns. That is a good metaphor for describing Cupid. Behind his beautiful face and body was a personality the gods and goddesses did not want to get close to. They were always wary of making him angry, because he might shoot them with one of his arrows, and they would end up being passionately in love with a cow, or a stone wall.

The Greek poet Sappho described Cupid as "bittersweet," while Hesiod, another Greek poet, wrote that Cupid "loosens the limbs and overpowers the good judgment of people and gods." I wish someone had brought Hesiod's words to my attention when I was fifteen. Maybe I would not have spent so much of my life with loose limbs. If my judgment about women had been any worse, I would have been arrested and put in jail with no possibility of parole.

As I can testify, Cupid cared about nothing except spreading lust and passion with his gold-tipped arrows, and pain and confusion with the lead-tipped ones. It did not matter to him if he created or destroyed relationships. It did not matter if the persons whom he infected with passion were exalted or crushed by the emotions that overwhelmed them. As long as passion and lust or pain and confusion reigned in the lives of mortals, Cupid was happy.

This was why Venus wanted him to take care of Psyche. No deity was better suited to carry out her revenge than her very own son, someone she could trust to do exactly as she wished.

She found Cupid in his basement woodworking shop, making a new set of arrows and tips. Arrows with tips of gold were dipped in a potion that infected mortals with the passions of love and lust. The arrows with leaden tips were dipped in another potion. These arrows turned lovers against each other and destroyed even memories of happiness in the most loving of couples.

Cupid had just completed making the new arrows and tips when Venus came in. "There's my darling boy!" she greeted him.

"Mother," Cupid responded warmly. He stopped what he was doing and gave her a hug and kiss. The two gazed into each other's eyes like lovers. I don't know about you, but I don't think that's the way mothers and sons are supposed to look at each other. But Venus was the only female in his life. Although he had a beautiful palace of his own hidden in a mountain valley of the Kingdom-by-the-Great-Blue-Sea, he spent scarcely any time there. Like a lot of men, he wanted to continue living at home and to be taken care of by his mother. This was fine with Venus. What she would do to the woman who tried to take him away from her would not be a pretty sight.

"I need a favor, son."

"Name it and it's yours. You know that."

"You are such a sweet boy."

"How could I not be, with a mother like you?"

Venus smiled. "There is a young woman in the Kingdom-by-the-Great-Blue-Sea. Her name is Psyche, a rather pretentious name for a mortal, if you ask me. She is very pretty, though in a rather plain and ordinary way. I suspect she is some kind of demon disguised as a mortal, because people are coming from all over to worship her as if she were, well, as if she were me. Have you ever heard anything so ridiculous in your life? Of course you haven't.

"Well, I can't allow this to continue. Could you make this Psyche fall in love with the most unlikely man in the entire kingdom, someone ugly beyond belief, someone who chews his food with his mouth open, snores loudly, and has no money? You get the idea. Would you do that for me, darling?"

"Consider it done, Mother."

"That's my sweet boy."

Cupid was surprised to see her forehead creased with tension and a nervous anxiousness in her eyes. He had never seen his mother so worried.

"Don't worry. Perhaps I'll make this imposter fall in love with a pig, or a large boulder. No one will want to worship her after they hear her declaiming love poems to a piece of stone."

Venus laughed, but her laugh was a little too loud and

went on for a little too long. "I'll be waiting eagerly for your return," she said in a tight voice.

"I'll take care of things this evening," he assured her.

Cupid wondered why his mother was so distressed about a mortal woman. How could the beauty of any woman condemned to die rival that of an immortal goddess, and especially that of Venus? The thought was ridiculous. And what kind of woman would dare allow herself to be compared to, and even mistaken for, the goddess of love? He would teach this Psyche a lesson she would never forget.

Cupid Gets Surprised

Night came. Cupid filled his quiver with an equal number of gold- and lead-tipped arrows and flew through the firmament that separated the back of the sky from the front. When he reached the Kingdom-by-the-Great-Blue-Sea, he glided easily above the rooftops, peering into windows until he saw a couple holding hands and kissing. He smiled, strung his bow with a lead-tipped arrow, and shot through the open window and into the breast of the woman. Immediately she pushed her husband away, exclaiming, "I'm sick of this. This is all you care about, all you want to do. You don't care about me at all. All you care about is sex!"

The husband looked as if he had just been slapped,

which, in a way, he had. "What just happened?" he asked, bewildered. "What did I do?"

Cupid chuckled quietly. "That's where their marriage was going, anyway. I just saved them from wasting a lot of time and energy getting there." Satisfied, he left to find Psyche.

The king's palace was in a meadow at the edge of a large grove of trees just outside the main village. The massive building was dark except for the dim yellow of candlelight from a window on the top floor, at the rear. As Cupid flew toward that light, he took his bow from around his shoulder and a gold-tipped arrow from the quiver. He landed softly on the roof above the room from which the light came. Just as he did, the double doors leading to the balcony opened and out came Psyche, wearing a long white gown as soft as starshine.

Cupid put the arrow against the bow's string. Although he had promised his mother that he would make Psyche fall in love with a hideous man, he knew Venus would be pleased if Psyche was made to appear ridiculous. How he managed to accomplish that was not important.

Psyche went to the balcony's edge and stared up into the night sky. Cupid pulled back on the bow. How much more ridiculous could he make her appear than if she were to be passionately in love with the night sky? All he needed her to do was turn around so he could place the arrow in her heart. But then she spoke:

"O beloved Venus!" she called out in a voice trembling with yearning. "Goddess, please help me. The people mistake me for you. Who could take your place? Certainly not I. I am not worthy to have my name said in the same breath as yours. Do not be angry with me, as nothing would make me happier than to be taken away from all the eyes that look at me with devotion and desire. Please, Goddess. Please help me."

Cupid's arm slowly came down and he released the tension on the bow. He could not believe what he had just heard her say. Those words could not have come from the person his mother had described. This one had no desire to take his mother's place in the hearts of the people. Perhaps there was another palace in the kingdom. But he knew there wasn't. Perhaps this was the good daughter, and somewhere else in the palace was the one of whom Venus had spoken. But, no. She had spoken of how people were mistaking her for Venus. She was Psyche.

Even if he had not understood her words, he would have been moved by her voice, which sounded as if it were singing though it uttered only words. Even Apollo could not coax sounds of such beauty from his lyre.

Was his mother mistaken? As hard as it was for him to believe that Venus could be wrong about anything, he believed she was in error this time. If she had heard Psyche's prayer, she would have seen how mistaken she was. But knowing his mother as he did, he was sure she had not been listening to Psyche's prayer, or anyone else's. Venus did not have much patience for the prayers of humans, especially prayers unaccompanied by offerings, and expensive ones.

He did not know what to do. Should he go ahead and make Psyche the laughingstock of the kingdom because he had promised his mother he would? Or should he go back to Olympus and tell his mother about Psyche and her prayer, tell his mother that she was wrong? Cupid tried to imagine telling Venus she was wrong about something. He wouldn't dare. But he shuddered to think what Venus would do if he disobeyed her.

He raised the bow once more and pulled back on it, waiting for Psyche to turn around. And she did.

She had large dark eyes, straight black hair that hung to her hips and shone like wisdom more ancient than time, a small nose and full lips contained in a heart-shaped face of fragile gentleness and strong sincerity.

She did not look up. If she had, she would have seen what appeared to be a statue of the god Cupid, poised to release an arrow into some mortal's heart. But she saw no one as she reentered her chambers and pulled the double doors closed behind her.

The sound of the doors closing caused Cupid to blink his eyes as if awakening from a spell. His arms came down slowly and he relaxed the tension on the bow. He returned the arrow to his quiver and slung the bow around his shoulder.

He could not believe what he had just seen. No wonder mortals thought she had come to replace Venus. To his amazement, she was, indeed, more beautiful than his mother. She was more beautiful than all the sunrises and sunsets that had been and would be.

A feeling of perfect peace began to permeate his body. For the first time in his eternal life, he wanted to be with someone besides his mother. He wanted to give himself to Psyche's beauty and, thereby, become as beautiful as she was.

Cupid did not understand what had happened to him. If you think about it, that's kind of funny. He was the god of love, but he had never been *in love*. Love had been a game to him, a game that he controlled with his bow and arrows. But after he saw Psyche, his life would never be again what it had been.

You're probably wondering the same thing I am. What did he see? Let me ask you. What do you and I see when we look at someone and we hear ourselves thinking:

"She is fine!"

"He's hot!"

"I want to get to know her."

"I've got to find a way to get him to talk to me."

Surely Cupid had seen many beautiful women and not been affected. What was different this time? I do not know. I asked the story if it knew, and it didn't. When I think about all the times I have fallen in love (and there have been many, thank Jupiter!), I can remember feeling like I had been startled awake from a sleep I had not known I was in.

Have you ever noticed how you feel more alive when you fall in love?

Maybe there are no words to explain what happened to Cupid and what happens to us. That's rather embarrassing for a storyteller like myself to admit. But because I am a storyteller, I know that all knowledge cannot be put into words. When our souls are touched by beauty, words give way to the vocabulary of silence. If we are wise, we submit to what can never be wholly explained or understood. However, if we turn away from the terrifying initiation into the kingdom of soul where beauty is all, we are refusing life.

What choice would Cupid make?

Cupid's Decision

As the god of love stood on the balcony trying to understand what was happening to him, there was the sound of soft knocking on the door to Psyche's room.

"Psyche?"

"Father?"

The door opened and in came a tall, thin man with a dark beard threaded with gray.

"To what do I owe the pleasure of a visit from you at such an hour of the night?"

The king sighed. "I have been unable to sleep. I fear your mother and I have done you a disservice by allowing you out only one day a month. Yet, when you went out every day, your beauty paralyzed the kingdom. I want to apologize for my inept handling of a complex situation."

"Thank you, Father. I am sorry for the attention I attract. My beauty is a burden for all of us. I wish I knew what it is people see and feel when they look at me. I know only loneliness since my sisters married and moved away. You and Mother are the only ones I have for company now. Everyone else is afraid to speak to me, to ask me even how I am. You have no idea, Father, how cruel beauty can be."

The king nodded. "Your mother and I wonder if we have angered Venus by permitting you to be an object of worship."

"Oh, Father! Mere moments ago I prayed to the goddess and asked her to forgive me if my beauty offended her."

"What would you think if I went to the shrine of the god Apollo and asked him to tell me what your future is to be?"

"Is that the wisest course?" Psyche asked, after a long pause. "Would it not be better to go to the shrine of Venus and beg her forgiveness?"

Outside, on the balcony, Cupid was shaking his head violently, and perhaps would have intervened if he had not heard the king say, "The goddess is a being of great passion, and anger is, perhaps, a greater passion even than love. When she is angry, the goddess can be more vicious than the three-headed dog Cerberus who guards the way to the underworld. But the god Apollo is not ruled by passion. And he is incapable of lying."

"What if he reveals my fate to be something I cannot bear?"

The king put his arms around his daughter and hugged her tightly. "Is it not better to know the truth, regardless?"

Psyche laid her head against her father's chest. "I suppose that is so," she whispered, "but that does not make me any less afraid."

Though she spoke softly, Cupid heard every word. His ears were keenly attuned to the words of the heart, and Psyche's heart was so sad he thought he could hear its tears. He wanted to take away her sadness and protect her from anyone and everything that could ever hurt her. But what would his mother say? She would . . . would—. He didn't want to imagine what she would do to him or Psyche. But what if Venus didn't know? When she found out, which she eventually would, what could she do then? She might be angry for a while, but that would not last long. His mother wanted him to be happy, and if Psyche was the one who made him happy, Venus would be grateful.

Inside Psyche's chambers the king and his daughter had said good night. Psyche blew out the candles and went to bed.

Cupid remained on the balcony, helpless to leave. He had never been concerned about anyone's well-being, but he cared about what happened to the one lying within. Not until Sun began pushing darkness beneath the western horizon did Cupid, reluctantly, take his leave from the sleeping and beautiful Psyche.

As he flew slowly toward Olympus, he was elated and confused, excited and afraid, awed and angry. Never had so many emotions held him enthralled. He, who had the power to control the lives of mortals and deities, had lost control of his own life. How could that be? How could hearing a voice and seeing a face transform his life so completely? All meaning resided now in a person to whom he had never addressed a word. That was ridiculous! Yet, it was also as true and real as birds' songs welcoming Sun to another day.

I know it's true, and so do you. I remember the first time I fell in love. It was my sophomore year in college. But wait! Did you hear what I said? I *fell* in love. We fall down, fall off a ladder, fall behind in doing something, but why do we *fall* in love? And from where do we *fall* when we *fall* in love? When we use this verb, are we trying to describe the accidental nature of the experience?

That day I fell in love for the first time, I did not wake up thinking, "I'm going to fall in love today." Love is not intentional. My intent that day was to go to the school library and get a book. I was going through the card catalog to see if the library had the book I wanted. I sensed a presence and looked around, and there she was! That was all it took. I saw her and my soul passed from me to her with all the certainty and finality of night changing to day. She had not yet seen me, but my life now had a meaning it had lacked in all the minutes leading to the one when I looked up and saw her. And all the moments before seemed like ones in which I had been scarcely awake. Now I was fully alive for the first time in my then-nineteen years. (And Sylvia fell in love with me. Whether it was in that instant when she, feeling my eyes on her, looked over at me, or days or weeks later, I do not know. Nor does it matter. It only matters that we held each other's souls for almost three years, but she wanted to marry and I did not. I still had a lot of falling in love to do.)

Like me and like you, Cupid accepted that it was not only possible but rational to love someone to whom he had not spoken—to love someone whose voice he had heard, whose face he had seen for, what? Five minutes? Ten? Certainly no more than that. Yet, this was all it took for him to feel as if he could lift mountains, polish stars, and hold the sun in his hands.

I'm going to get philosophical for a moment since this is a philosophical novel. In love, and perhaps only in love, are the finite limitations of self dissolved and we merge, not only with the beloved other, but with wonder itself. In love, whether it is love of another, of music, art, or whatever, we belong to someone or something and are no longer alone.

Cupid had not known he was alone and lonely. But now that he had joined his aloneness with that of another, though she did not know it yet, he was hers as surely as a smile on her lips was hers.

In joy and gratitude, Cupid laughed. His laughter rolled

from one end of the dawning sky to the other, and mortals smiled in their sleep.

Cupid and Venus Talk

As Cupid passed through the firmament and entered Olympus, he had two tasks. One was to talk to Venus. She would probably be a little upset that he had not done anything to Psyche. However, he was sure she would understand after he explained that Psyche was not a threat to her. The task he dreaded was talking to Apollo.

Venus was waiting anxiously in her chambers for Cupid's return, and when she heard his footsteps in the corridor, she flung open the door.

"My son!"

"Mother."

Venus had never seen such a beautiful smile on Cupid's face. "Your face tells me you must have devised something deliciously fiendish for that imposter. So tell me! What did you do to Psyche?"

Standing before his mother, seeing her look of eager anticipation, Cupid frowned as he realized that telling her might not be as easy as he had thought.

"Is something the matter?" she wanted to know. "Are you all right?"

"I'm fine, Mother. It's just that, well, Psyche is not trying to take your place. Did you hear her prayer?"

"Of course I did," Venus snapped. "Don't tell me you believed what she said?"

"Didn't you?"

"Of course not. She's more clever than I gave her credit for. But if she thinks that little bit of acting is going to persuade me to withhold my wrath, she is mistaken!"

Cupid could not believe what he was hearing. "But Mother. I was there. I saw her as she prayed to you. She was not acting."

Venus glared at her son. "Are you telling me you didn't do as I asked?"

"I-I thought you would have changed your mind after hearing her prayer," he responded fearfully.

Venus shook her head in dismay. "I can't believe you allowed yourself to be taken in by her! But that merely shows how powerful she is. If she was able to fool you, her powers to deceive are greater than I could have imagined. Now that you know the truth, I'm sure you will do as your mother asked you to."

"Why don't you believe me?" Cupid asked with fervent sincerity. "I was there. I saw her as she prayed to you. I heard her tell her father how devoted she was to you. You have nothing to fear from her. She adores you!"

Venus gave Cupid an indulgent smile. "You may be the god of love, but you do not know the wiles and ways of women, how they can ensnare a male, even a god, it appears, by their pretenses. I know women far better than you ever will. You must not let yourself be taken in by her.

Seeing the effect she has had on you, it is imperative that you make sure she never again uses her magic on god or mortal."

In all of his eternal life there had never been and never would be another moment like this one. Cupid had to choose which truth meant more to him—the truth of his love for his mother, or this new truth with its promise of a beauty that would unfold, evermore and evermore. But he did not choose truth. Cupid lied. "Of course I will do as you ask, Mother." With those words, words he had no intention of abiding by, he betrayed himself and his love for Psyche and bound himself more tightly to his mother.

Venus smiled and kissed him on the cheek, then turned and walked away, ignoring the look of sadness on his face. Cupid was disappointed that he had not been able to share with his mother this new and strange joy, this ecstatic confusion, the bewildering awe enthralling him. But he did not want to disappoint his mother. However, as he left her chambers, he was disappointed with himself for caring more about her feelings than his own.

It is fearful to merge one's spirit with that of another's. This is why the beginning of relationships can be fraught with terror. Love requires courage, and I am sad to say, Cupid was a coward. In lying to his mother, he was choosing to keep secret his soul's love. True, he kept his mother's love, but he placed himself in danger of losing something of greater value—himself. However, we must be fair to him.

He was new to love. He did not know how much courage love required.

Cupid was not accustomed to emotions of disappointment and self-loathing. So he ignored these feelings that might have forced him to stand up to his mother and tell her that he loved Psyche. Instead he convinced himself that by lying, he had mollified Venus. Now he had to confront Apollo, that most formidable of the deities, who would not be as easy to handle as his mother had been.

Apollo and Daphne

Cupid had every reason to worry about meeting with Apollo. He was a god of enormous powers. His realm consisted of the arts as well as prophecy, which was why Psyche's father was going to consult him. He was the god of healing, too, though he could also bring on plagues. Last but by no means least, he was the god of archery, which brought Cupid to the problem. Apollo hated him and, as far as Cupid was concerned, for no good reason.

Back when Cupid was still a boy, a giant serpent named Python was terrorizing everybody and everything. Apollo had killed Python with one shot from his bow and arrow. He took great pride in his feat and was not shy about recounting it to everybody, more than once.

One afternoon Apollo was sitting on Venus's porch,

telling her how he had killed Python with a single, well-placed arrow. Having heard the story more times than she cared to remember, Venus wasn't listening. She was trying to decide whether she wanted the peach-colored or spring green silk sheets put on her bed for the night. She had new sheets put on her bed every evening because, well, because she was Venus and the thought of sleeping on the same sheets two nights in a row was so upsetting that she almost needed to get in the hot tub to relieve the stress of such an idea.

Suddenly, she became aware that Apollo was laughing. What had happened? Apollo did not laugh, having no sense of humor that anyone had ever been able to find. Venus noticed him pointing at Cupid, who had just come onto the porch with his bow and quiver to go practice.

"Well, well, well. Isn't this cute?" Apollo laughed again. He picked up his enormous bow from the floor beside his chair. "With this bow and an arrow, I killed Python, a serpent who had been terrorizing everyone and whose girth covered many acres across the plains. Little boy, what do you think you can do with that tiny bow and those tiny arrows?" His manner turned serious. "The bow and arrow are *my* weapons. Find something else to amuse yourself with."

Venus saw Cupid's eyes narrow.

"Apollo? I think you should apologize to Cupid. He doesn't like being made fun of," Venus said, great concern in her voice.

Apollo looked at her scornfully. "Apologize to a child? Surely, you speak in jest."

"Apollo. Dear. You don't understand. I really think you should apologize. You obviously don't know my son."

"I'm sure he can do many wonderful things that gladden his mother's heart, but I am Apollo. What could this child possibly do to me?"

"*Oy vey,*" Venus said quietly. "Don't say I didn't warn you."

Cupid had already strung his bow with a gold-tipped arrow. Then in a voice that was more like a man's than a child's, he said to Apollo, "Your bow and arrow have power over that which is without. Mine has power over that which is within." He pulled on the bow and let the arrow go straight into Apollo's heart. At that instant, Daphne, the beautiful nymph, daughter of Peneus the river god, came into Apollo's view. Quickly Cupid took an arrow tipped with lead and shot it into her heart.

The eyes of Apollo and Daphne met. Love gripped Apollo like the talons of an eagle piercing the warm, quivering flesh of a rabbit. But enmity claimed Daphne's heart. Apollo looked at her with love-filled eyes; Daphne regarded him with cold hatred. Apollo saw the revulsion on her face, but he was certain that, in time, she would come to love him as much as he loved her.

But he was wrong. The potion from Cupid's arrow coursed through Daphne's veins and chilled any warmth she might have felt for Apollo, or any man. The very thought of being responsible for a man's emotions disgusted her. Why would a woman allow herself to become entangled in men's feelings and desires? The idea of a man touching her body was repulsive. If she had thought Jupiter would take her seriously, she would have asked him to decree marriage a crime, and any man who approached a woman with even the thought of marriage would be sent into exile. But she knew that Jupiter's love of women rendered him incapable of understanding how she felt.

Poor Daphne. Every time she looked around, there was Apollo with that pitiful look on his face men get when they fall in love. He followed her from the time she got up in the morning until she went to bed at night, and then he slept on the ground outside her bedroom window.

Apollo was probably the first stalker in history, except, back in those days, people didn't know anything about stalking, which is why Daphne didn't go to the police and get a restraining order against him. The only defense she had was to run as fast as she could every time she saw him staring at her like a cocker spaniel wanting to come in out of the rain.

The day came when Daphne had enough. She stepped outside her house that particular morning and there was Apollo, standing in the yard with a bunch of wildflowers he had picked himself, and a *big* basket of chocolates. The sight of all that chocolate was tempting. A woman will put up with a whole lot from a man if he keeps her supplied with chocolate. But as much as Daphne loved chocolate, it wasn't enough to make her forget how much she hated feeling a man's emotion reaching out for her like a vine seeking a tree to wrap itself around.

"Go away! Leave me alone!" she yelled at Apollo.

Instead of doing what she asked, he started reciting a love poem he had gotten Erato, the muse of literature, to write for him. Now, I know you men think women go for poetry. Some do, but a whole lot don't. You could be reciting your poetry and the young lady will look like she's interested, when what she's thinking is "What's up with the poetry, and how many other girls has he read that poem to?" However, I will tell you two things no woman can resist. Number two is cook dinner for her. Women get weak in the knees when they find out a man can cook. But number one works even better than that. If a woman knows you listen to her and take seriously what she says, she will give you her heart, body, and soul. It is obvious that Apollo was retarded when it came to listening. He kept hearing *yes* when she was saying *no.*

Daphne took off running. She was fast, but she had never run as fast as she did that morning. She was determined to get away from Apollo once and for all. She might have done so if Cupid had not been watching. He saw that Apollo was tiring and was falling farther and farther behind Daphne. So what did Cupid do? He shot another arrow into Apollo, which gave him new energy.

Daphne thought she had outrun Apollo. She stopped and looked back, expecting to see him standing in the road, trying to catch his breath. Instead he was running faster than ever, and if she didn't do something, he was going to catch her. Daphne would rather die than become the property of a man.

She called out to her father, Peneus. "Save me, Father! Make the earth open up and swallow me, or change me into something so I can escape this danger."

No sooner had she spoken than her body became stiff. Bark began growing on her legs, abdomen, breasts, and face, and her hair turned to leaves. Apollo reached her just as her transformation into a tree was completed.

Apollo looked at the tree and saw how graceful and beautiful it was. He put his arms around it.

"Henceforward, this shall be my tree," he declared. "I will wear your leaves in a wreath around my head. Emperors will wear wreaths of your leaves around their heads when they parade in triumph through the streets. Because I am eternally young, so shall you be also. Your leaves will always be green and never get old and fall to the ground."

And to this day, wreaths are made from the leaves of the laurel tree.

Since then, Cupid had made a point of staying out of Apollo's way, even at the semiannual Gods and Goddesses Solstice Banquet and Dance, when everyone drank so much mulled nectar that even Jupiter and Juno didn't quarrel.

Now Cupid had to go to Apollo's palace and convince

him to tell the king what Cupid wanted him to say. But Apollo couldn't lie. Well, if Cupid had his way—and he would—this was one time Apollo was going to lie.

Cupid Meets with Apollo

Of all the palaces on Olympus, Apollo's was the largest. It had to be, because he was responsible for so many activities. The palace stood at the center of Olympus. It had a round central building with passageways radiating from it to other buildings like the threads in a spider's web. The complex was made of long, dark slabs of the unknowable future, while the central building was composed of pale red slivers of hope.

Cupid tried to stay away from the center of Olympus, and not only because he was afraid of encountering Apollo. He also wanted to avoid Jupiter, who, if he saw Cupid, would ask him to shoot a golden arrow into the heart of every woman Jupiter desired. Cupid did not think he could make that many arrows.

As he began walking up the broad steps to Apollo's palace, he smiled at the cacophony of sounds coming from within—women singing, playing instruments, and loudly declaiming poetry. Cupid remembered seeing an item in the Olympus weekly newsletter, which said that the nine muses were coming for their semiannual conference, where they shared with each other and Apollo what they had inspired humans to create in the past six months. At the end of the week, there would be an arts festival, where they would perform for all the inhabitants of Olympus and invited guests.

Cupid liked the muses. Like him, they were winged, and several times a year, he and they would take a day or two off from their respective duties and go flying for the sheer joy of it. He was also fond of them because they provided the songs, poetry, and dances used by the lovers who had been struck by one of his gold-tipped arrows.

When Cupid entered Apollo's palace, he saw in front of him a broad staircase to the second floor. To his right and left were hallways leading to the many wings of the palace.

From the first hallway on his left, he identified the voice of Calliope singing as Euterpe's flute played a lovely harmonic line. His attention was then drawn to the third corridor on his right, where someone was singing a dirge-like melody while two others recited poetry.

The voices sounded familiar to Cupid, but it was a moment before he recognized Melpomene's voice singing, and Terpsichore and Erato declaiming poetry.

Hearing nothing coming from the hallway to his immediate left, Cupid decided to see if Apollo might be in one of the rooms there. When he opened the door at the hallway's end, he found himself in a large room whose floor was covered with papers so deep that they came to his knees. Clio, the muse of history, sat at a desk in the center of the room, writing furiously. As she finished each sheet of paper, she pushed it to the floor and continued writing on the next.

Cupid left quietly and went back along the hallway until he noticed a door was ajar. He peeked inside. Thalia, muse of comedy, sat in a window seat, chuckling at Polymnia, muse of mime, in the center of the room. He watched, transfixed, as Polymnia placed the palms of her hands against the air as if she were touching a wall. He could not remember how many times he had seen Polymnia act as if she were trapped within the four walls of a room. No matter how many times he saw her do this, he still did not understand how she was able to make him see a wall when none existed. Shaking his head, he returned to the entranceway and went down the hallway directly across from the one he had just explored.

He opened the door of the first room he came to and looked inside. The walls of this room were covered with lists of diseases and the names of the herbs that would cure the disease or relieve the discomfort of the symptoms. The room itself was filled with long tables on which lay piles of herbs, plants, and roots. At each table young men and women sat, filling bottles and jars.

Cupid left and went to the doors of the other rooms, but these were all locked. This was probably where Apollo kept the plagues and pestilences that he periodically set loose on mortals when he became bored with them.

Returning again to the entranceway, Cupid decided to go up to the next floor. Here, too, he found himself in a large round area with hallways radiating from it. In the first room off the corridor to his right he saw Urania, muse of astronomy. She was looking out the window and through the veil that kept mortals from seeing Olympus but through which the deities could see the world. Down there it was night, and Cupid watched as Urania pointed her finger at something with one hand and wrote with the other.

"What are you doing?" he asked.

"I'm naming every star in the night sky of the mortals."

"That's a big job! It'll take forever."

"Well, how much time do you think I have?"

"You have a point. I hate to interrupt, but would you happen to know where Apollo is?"

"He saw you coming up the steps and got upset. I've never seen him so agitated. He's afraid you're coming to shoot another one of your arrows into his heart."

Cupid smiled. "Oh, really."

"Really! He's in his chambers across the hall."

"Thanks. May I ask you a question?"

"Sure."

"Why are you telling me this?"

"Oh, to get back at him for making me muse of astronomy. Do you know how hard it is to come up with a name for every star?"

"I don't understand. Why do the stars need names?"

Urania looked surprised. "When they want to talk to

each other, don't you think they get tired of saying 'Hey, you!' and having ten billion stars all shout, 'Who? Me?'"

"Why don't you have the stars name themselves?"

Urania thought for a moment. "I never thought of that. That's a great idea. You have no idea how hard this job is. Just last week I lost my place and couldn't figure out for the life of me whether I had named this one particular star or not. I think there's a star without a name and one with two names—Theodorokus Alleppo. I hate it when I lose my place like that. Thanks for the idea. I'm going to go ask the stars what they think about it."

Without another word, Urania flew out the window and down to the veil and into the night heavens.

Cupid crossed the hallway and knocked on the door Urania had indicated.

There was no answer. He knocked again. No answer. Cupid tried the door. It opened. He entered quietly, closing the door behind him.

He found himself in another large room. The four walls were shelves filled with scrolls. In the center of the room was a long table. It, too, was covered with scrolls. Cupid picked up an unusually thick one and unrolled it. Inside was a note from Erato: *Lord Apollo. I inspired a blind man named Homer to write this. I think you will enjoy it.*

Cupid moved the note aside to read the title: *The Odyssey.*

Cupid was not much of a reader, especially if it was a long scroll, and this was the longest one he'd ever seen.

He set it back on the table and the scroll rerolled itself. He opened another one, on which was a note from Clio.

"Lord Apollo. Here is the account of the Peloponnesian War by Thucydides. I thought I had inspired him to give an objective account of the war, but I fear this is very one-sided. Inspiring humans to write the truth about their history takes every bit of strength I have, and quite frankly, I don't know if it's worth it. I want to put in for some vacation time. I would like to go back in time to the Egyptians. People who wrote in pictures did not lie because it took too much work. Is it all right that I asked for vacation time in a note? Or would you prefer I fill out the Request for Extended Vacation Time form?"

Cupid put the scroll down. He had to get on with what he came to do. Just then he heard someone trying to stifle a cough. The sound had come from a room in the back of Apollo's chambers.

This room, too, was filled with scrolls, but Cupid only gave them a cursory glance. However, he did notice one with a note attached: "For J. S. Bach. Mass in B Minor. Do not open until 1749." He had no idea what that meant.

"Apollo? I know you're in here."

There was a long silence, and then Apollo emerged sheepishly from a closet.

"I don't know why you're here and I don't want to know! Just stay away from me," Apollo said firmly.

"It's all right. I came on business."

"And what could that be? After what you did to me, I can't imagine what kind of business we could have with each other."

"Hold on. Don't blame me. If you hadn't made fun of me, nothing would have happened. My mother warned you."

If there's one thing the gods share with us humans, it is hating to admit when they are in the wrong. Apollo thought for a moment, trying to find a way to get out of losing face to Cupid. He considered the matter from the front side and the back, up, down, and sideways, and when he finished, things still looked the same.

Finally, he cleared his throat and, in a soft, barely audible voice, said, "Well, as loath as I am to admit it, your statement might have some merit. I suppose in my boasting about slaying Python, I might have needed to be taught a lesson."

Cupid smiled. "I appreciate what you said. As far as I'm concerned, bygones are bygones. I came to talk to you about some here-comes."

Apollo had no idea what Cupid was talking about. "Speak and tell me what brings you here."

Cupid told him about Psyche and her father's plans to learn Psyche's future from Apollo what was in Psyche's future. "When the king comes, I would like you to tell him she is to marry me."

Apollo said, "You know I can do nothing but tell the truth about what I see."

Cupid made as if to take his bow from around his torso.

Apollo quickly added, "However, what I see in a person's future is all a matter of how I interpret what I see."

"Thanks, Apollo. If there's ever anything I can do for you, don't hesitate to get in touch."

Apollo narrowed his eyes. "Tell me. How does your mother feel about your infatuation with a mortal?"

Cupid blushed. "I-I haven't gotten around to telling her yet."

"You what?" Apollo laughed. "I don't believe it. You're afraid of your mother."

"You won't tell, will you?" Cupid whispered.

"If you promise to never again strike me with one of your arrows."

Cupid shook his head and gave an evil smile. "I don't make deals like that. If you say a word to Venus, I will see to it that one of my arrows is in your heart until the end of eternity."

Apollo nodded quickly. "OK, OK. I won't say anything to Venus and I'll see what I can do about Psyche."

"Thanks, Apollo. And I mean it."

Psyche's Fate

When the king entered Psyche's chambers the following morning, he saw her standing at a window, looking down at the crowds waiting eagerly for her to make an appearance. He could see the stiff stillness of apprehension in her body.

"What have I done to you?" he asked quietly.

Psyche turned around.

The king saw tears in her eyes. "I have put the wants and needs of others above yours."

"You are the king," Psyche responded. "The needs of your subjects must take precedence over your own needs and even those of your family."

The king nodded. "But am I required to sacrifice the well-being and happiness of my youngest daughter?"

Psyche smiled weakly. "The king's youngest hopes not."

"So does the king. I am off to the shrine of Apollo. Are you prepared to obey the god's decree?"

"How can I know until I've heard the decree?"

"What the god decrees, we must obey."

"And if I refuse?"

"The god will mete out punishment on us all."

"Am I never to have a choice? Is my life always to be governed by what my father or a god deems best?"

The king had never seen anger on the face of his daughter or heard rebellion in her voice. He wondered if he really knew this child of his. Ashamed, he realized he had never sat and talked with her about what she wanted her life to be. She was a princess, the daughter of the king and queen. She was born to carry out the duties of her station. But what if she did not want to? What then?

Not knowing what to say, the king muttered, "I must

go. I will return after sunset to tell you of the god's decree. I hope his words will gladden your heart."

"I, too, Father. I, too."

Psyche was convinced it was the longest day that had ever been. The sun seemed to take a week to climb to the top of the sky, only to stay there another week before beginning its slide downward to the bed of night.

Finally, evening came. Psyche heard, or thought she did, the hoofbeats of the king's horse and those of his counselors. She waited anxiously for her father to come and reveal her fate as Apollo had decreed it.

But the king did not come that night.

From Olympus, Cupid had seen the king return, his head slumped to his chest as if he were grieving. Something was wrong! "What in Juno's name did Apollo tell him?" Cupid wondered aloud. Obviously it was not what Cupid had asked him to say.

Cupid flew quickly down to the palace and to the roof above Psyche's chambers. He waited eagerly for the king to come and tell Psyche what Apollo had said. But the hours passed without any sign of the king.

Wondering what was wrong, Cupid flew around the palace until he saw the king and queen sitting alone before the large fireplace in the Great Hall. They were staring into the low-burning fire as if someone had died.

Had Apollo decreed Psyche's death? If he had, Cupid would have Apollo reciting love poetry to his toenails with all the gods and goddesses for an audience!

Another day passed, and still the king did not come to Psyche. After yet another day went by without a visit from the king, Psyche knew Apollo had decreed what she feared most, that she belonged to all those who needed her beauty. She would spare her father the pain of telling her that which he knew would lead her to take her life.

She opened the doors to the balcony and walked to the railing. From the roof above, Cupid watched, horrified, as she sat on the railing, then pulled her legs over. She was going to kill herself! He was just about to spread his wings and fly down to catch her as she fell, but just then the door of her chamber opened.

"Psyche!" the king called out. "Psyche!"

She turned around. "Father?"

"Psyche, please come inside. It is not as you feared."

"It isn't?"

"No. Please. Come inside."

Psyche swung her legs around and went back into the room. Outside, Cupid breathed a sigh of relief. Then he alighted quietly on the balcony, hid next to the doors, and listened.

"What did Apollo say?" Psyche asked eagerly.

"The god said that I am to take you to the highest

mountain, where your husband—." The king faltered and stopped.

"My husband? Please, Father. Go on. What about my husband?"

"Your husband," the king continued in a broken voice, "an evil and destructive monster, will take you for his wife."

Father and daughter were silent for a moment. Then Psyche started crying softly.

"I am sorry I did not come to you at once and tell you," the king apologized. "But I was devastated and could scarcely speak."

He put his arms around her and they both wept.

Outside, Cupid fumed. "An evil and destructive monster. Is that what you think I am, Apollo? I'll show you what evil and destruction are!" But he stopped when he realized that Apollo had merely put his own little twist on what Cupid had asked him to say. It did not matter how Apollo described him as long as Psyche was going to be his and his alone!

Immediately, Cupid flew from the palace. He had a lot to do.

Psyche's Wedding Day

When Sun awoke the following morning, he knew immediately: something was wrong. Earth was not singing and welcoming him back to the land where Psyche lived, something Earth had done since the day of her birth. But on this morning, as Sun rose over Earth's eastern edge, she was not singing but weeping:

"Brother Sun! Brother Sun!" Earth called out as Sun's first rays began pushing darkness to its lair on the other side of the world. "Do not lend your light to this horrible day! Our Psyche, beloved Psyche, is being sent away to become the bride of an evil and destructive monster, and we will never see her again."

Sun stopped rising. How was he supposed to live if he could not gaze upon Psyche each day? Unlike people who only saw her for a few minutes one afternoon each month, Sun saw her every day from the moment she awoke. Only the sight of her beauty at the beginning of each day gave him the strength to climb the sky. People did not understand how hard Sun had to work to make his way up to the very top of the sky without a ladder to walk on, or rope to climb with. Some days Sun was so out of breath and tired by the time he got over to the western part of the world, he went to bed wondering if he could get up the next morning. Many days he would not have except for the fact that he wanted to see Psyche.

Sun knew there was nothing he could do to save Psyche, but that did not mean he had to watch. But how could he not? He saw everything that happened on Earth. He needed something between him and Earth, something big enough and thick enough that he could not see through it.

The answer came immediately. He needed the help of Aeolus, the mortal who controlled the Four Winds. Sun aimed a strong beam into the cave where Aeolus lived with his wife, Cyane, and the Four Winds.

"Greetings, my friend," Sun began when Aeolus came outside. "I don't know if you have heard the news, but this is a sad day. Psyche is to be married to an evil monster, and I can't bear to witness such a sad event."

"That is sad indeed," Aeolus commiserated. "Her beauty brings joy to so many. Is there nothing we can do?"

"For her, no. For me, perhaps. Because of where you live, you will be spared the sight of her leaving the kingdom. I need your help so I will be spared the sight, also."

"I will do anything I can," Aeolus offered.

"I am grateful. I was wondering if the Four Winds could bring together all the clouds and blow them over the Kingdom-by-the-Great-Blue-Sea? In that way I will be hidden behind the clouds and will not see what happens to Psyche."

Aeolus hesitated. "I don't know. I'll have to talk to the Winds, because they are the ones who will have to do all the work. You are asking a lot."

"I understand."

"And Favonius, West Wind, had a big argument a while back with Aquilo, North Wind, and moved out."

Aeolus went back inside the cave and told Aquilo, Auster (South Wind), and Eurus (East Wind), what Sun wanted of them. The Winds were saddened by the news of

Psyche's fate. She had danced and played in the palace garden with them. Each of them had blown through her hair, stroked her arms, and been rewarded with a smile of such sweetness that when any of the Winds thought of blowing through the kingdom as a storm, they went to another kingdom instead. They could not do anything that would turn her smile to sorrow. Understanding how Sun felt, they went quickly to work.

From his new home at the western edge of the world, Favonius saw his siblings blowing the clouds. When they told him what had happened and what they were doing, he began blowing the clouds in his western sphere toward the Kingdom-by-the-Great-Blue-Sea.

Soon the sky over the kingdom was filled with dark clouds so thick and heavy that Sister Moon, thinking she had overslept, started to get out of bed. But then she noticed that Evening Star was still snoring quietly, and she was always up before Sister Moon.

"Why is it so dark?" Sister Moon asked aloud.

"That's Brother Sun's doing," answered North Star, who never slept. "The Four Winds have covered him with every cloud in the heavens, and he's hiding behind them, bawling like he's never going to shine again. I believe he's having a nervous breakdown."

"Serves him right!" Sister Moon mumbled and got back under the covers. She and Brother Sun had a long courtship once, and it looked like they were going to get married. But then Brother Sun saw Psyche for the first time. After that, he didn't have eyes for anybody else. But if the truth be known, Sister Moon had never understood how she and Brother Sun would have stayed married since she liked to be out and about when he was sleeping, and he was raring to go when she was getting ready for bed. It would not have been much of a marriage.

In the Kingdom-by-the-Great-Blue-Sea word spread that Psyche was going to be married to a monster! It would have been devastating enough to learn that Psyche was going to marry, but that her husband was a monster? This was more than the people could bear. Each of them had a picture in his and her mind of what the monster looked like. For some he was a dragon whose every exhalation was smoke and fire. For others he was a giant with a single eye in his forehead. Still others imagined a wizened old man with a large nose, and warts the size of dinosaur eggs all over his face.

Whatever the monster looked like, all agreed that Psyche was being consigned to a life of misery and suffering, and the people wailed and sobbed. Their grief was so great that flowers wilted, and though it was spring, trees dropped their green leaves. Birds refused to sing; fish stopped swimming; and lions and lambs wept on each other's shoulders.

Alone in her chambers, Psyche could hear the outpouring of grief and was moved by it. We only grieve the loss of those we love. Had she been mistaken? Had the people genuinely loved her, or were they grieving because they would never gaze on her beauty again? Perhaps it was a little of both.

She had always felt unworthy of such ardent attention, because she had done nothing to merit it. Her beauty was a gift bestowed on her in the womb. Perhaps that did not matter. As her father had said: The experience of her beauty brought a transcendent pleasure to their spirits and softened their hearts as nothing else ever had or would. Beauty had been put into her keeping as if it were a child she was to care for. Tears came to her eyes as she understood: she had failed in not accepting the gift of beauty.

And she wept.

Meanwhile Cupid was flying to the home of Favonius, that most gentle of winds, West Wind. It took him all morning and into the early afternoon to fly to the forest of tall trees on the rim of the western horizon where Favonius now lived. Cupid arrived just as Favonius was getting ready to take a nap on the tops of the trees.

"Greetings, Favonius."

Favonius's eyes opened wide as he recognized Cupid. "Greetings, god. To what do I owe the honor of a visit from one such as you?"

"I have a favor to ask."

"Not you, too," Favonius replied.

"What do you mean?"

"I'm about to take a nap because I'm tired out from doing a favor for Brother Sun. He had me and my three siblings busy this morning."

"Doing what?"

"Blowing every cloud in the world over the Kingdom-by-the-Great-Blue-Sea."

"Ah! That explains it. When I went to the cave of Aeolus, looking for you, I wondered why your siblings were lying on the floor panting for breath. What did Sun want with so many clouds?"

"They are blocking his view so he doesn't have to see Psyche get married to a monster."

Cupid smiled to himself. "Is that so? Well, I hope you aren't too tired that you can't carry out my request."

"What is it you want me to do?"

After Cupid told him, Favonius smiled. "That will be a pleasure! A pleasure, indeed!"

"Thank you," Cupid responded. "Now I must go and make preparations."

Psyche scarcely noticed as her servants bathed her and rubbed her body with oils so she would smell like a field of flowers for her husband. Her servants brushed her long hair until it glowed like deepest night. Finally, they dressed her in a long white gown. Then they left, tears in their eyes, suppressed sobs in their throats.

"Your tears are too late," Psyche said quietly. "You should have cried when the people were calling me the new

Venus. You should have cried when they abandoned the goddess's temples to look upon me. My marriage to a monster is the goddess punishing me. But if this is my fate, I will try to meet it as bravely as I can."

On Olympus, Venus was growing angry. She had been waiting and waiting for Cupid to return and tell her that she no longer had to be concerned about Psyche. But she had not seen him, and nobody knew where he was. Venus remembered Cupid's smile when he came back from where she'd sent him to make Psyche's existence a horror. How could she have been so obtuse as not to have realized what that smile was about? But no. It was unthinkable that her son would have betrayed her and fallen in love with the mortal she hated more than anyone. However, if he had, it was only because Psyche had cast a spell on him.

If only she could see Earth, she might find out where Psyche was and what she was doing. But the clouds over the Kingdom-by-the-Great-Blue-Sea were as thick as illness and prevented her from seeing anything. As if that were not bad enough, someone had been crying most of the day. No one ever cried on Olympus, but the sound was unmistakable.

Everything combined had put Venus in as bad a mood as she had ever been in. Someone was going to suffer, and since she could not find Psyche, she could at least find whoever was doing all that crying.

Venus followed the sound of the weeping to the backside of Olympus. There she saw Brother Sun sitting, his legs hanging over the side, his head bowed. He was crying so hard, his tears were putting out his light. If he kept crying, he would drown his light, and gods and mortals would be left with nothing but moonlight, starshine, and nightglow.

"Brother Sun? What is your problem?" Venus asked, none too politely.

"Psyche is leaving us, to marry a monster."

Venus's face broke into the first smile she'd had all day. "Is that so?" she asked, making no attempt to hide the pleasure in her voice.

"I don't think I'll ever shine again," Sun went on.

Venus kicked Sun in his rear. "You best get on your way. And stop all that crying! If you're not careful, you *will* put your light out, and we'll really be in a mess then. Go do your job!"

Reluctantly, Brother Sun resumed his arduous climb to the top of the sky.

Venus was pleased to learn that this was Psyche's wedding day, but she wanted to see the ceremony for herself. She had to do something about all the clouds blocking her view of Earth.

She sent for Aeolus. Several hours passed before he came to her palace. His clothes were disheveled, his hair uncombed, and he was so tired he could scarcely keep his eyes open.

"What's going on, Aeolus? You look a mess!"

"I'm having problems with my children. My son Aquilo, North Wind, has turned out to be evil."

"What does he do?"

"He waits until the weather is cold and there's snow and ice on the ground. Then he blows as hard as he can. I don't know how many times I told him that people need a cool breeze when the weather is hot, not when it's cold. He said he likes to see people shiver. And my youngest boy, Favonius, he moved out. Went to live with some trees. Said he was tired of living in a cave with the rest of us. And if that wasn't bad enough, Sun woke me up first thing this morning and told me to have my children bring all the clouds in the sky to hang over the Kingdom-by-the-Great-Blue-Sea. I tried to tell him that some of the clouds were just about ready to drop rain on the crops of folks on the other side of the world, who need rain bad. He said he didn't care about that. And now, just as me and my wife were finally good and asleep, here comes one of your servants saying you want to see me in a hurry. Well, here I am. What do you want? And it better be good, because Cyane does not like to have her beauty sleep interrupted."

"I want you to take the clouds away."

"What! I can't do that. Not after Brother Sun had me bring them over here."

"Can't one of your children blow enough away so I can see what's going on down there?"

Aeolus shook his head. "I'm sorry. My children are tired and all out of breath. People will be lucky if they get their breath back in time to blow summer up from the southern climes."

Venus frowned. She did not like anyone refusing to do what she wanted.

Aeolus looked at her. "You can make faces all you want, but I'll tell you the truth. If I go back down there and wake my boys up and tell them you want the clouds blown away, I'm afraid they will up and leave me. And I could not handle that right now. But I can tell you that—"

"Men!" Venus sneered, interrupting him. "Get out! You're worthless to me!"

Aeolus opened his mouth to finish the sentence, but Venus interrupted him again. "I said, get out! I don't want to hear any more lame excuses!"

Aeolus shrugged. He thought the goddess would have wanted to hear that Favonius was going to play an important role in the marriage of Cupid to Psyche, something Favonius had been so proud of, he had made a special visit to the cave to tell Aeolus. But if Venus didn't want to hear what he had to say, he'd keep his mouth shut. Aeolus called for a playful breeze and was taken back to his cave.

The Wedding Processional

It was early afternoon, around the time of day when Psyche used to walk from the palace to the village and back. This afternoon, though, she would walk through the village and into the unknown.

Clouds more dense than anyone had ever seen blocked

Sun's light, submerging the Kingdom-by-the-Great-Blue-Sea into a gravelike gloom.

Outside the palace, people lined both sides of the road. They held torches so they could see Psyche for the last time. No one spoke. There was the occasional sound of weeping and sniffling, and then the silence returned as thick and heavy as unshed tears.

This reminds me of my weddings. At all six of them, the bride cried; her mother and her sisters cried; and, in fact, every woman there cried. The first couple of times, I got mad because I thought they were crying because the bride was marrying me! But I eventually understood; marriage is different for women. No matter how much a woman loves the man she is going to marry, a part of her is terrified. For a woman, marriage is a journey into the dark unknown, and she doesn't know what might be hiding in the darkness. Maybe more couples would stay together if men accompanied their brides into the unknown and, once there, began again.

Psyche sat on a stone bench in the palace garden. "Is this what it is like to die?" she wondered. She was leaving everything and everyone she had ever known and would never see them again.

She was glad the very day looked as if it wanted to weep. It would have been cruel had the sun been pouring down its warm light when she felt as cold as the moon.

Psyche heard the gates to the garden open. She stood up and turned. Her parents were walking toward her. She embraced first her mother, then her father. The three stood in silence, the parents gazing into their daughter's face, and she into theirs. They had tears in their eyes, but no one cried.

Finally, the king said, "It is time."

They left the garden and walked in silence along a corridor until they came to the great doors of the palace. The three paused. They wanted to say something, but their minds were too numbed for even a letter of the alphabet to say its name to them.

Finally, Psyche looked at the guards, nodded once, and they slowly pulled open the heavy doors. She took a deep breath, exhaled slowly, and walked out without a backward glance at the palace. In front of her went four of the king's soldiers, each holding a torch high. The king and queen walked behind Psyche, guarded on each side by a soldier with a torch. Behind them came four more soldiers also holding torches.

Psyche walked slowly, her head held high. She looked into the faces of the people lining the road—something she had never done—and saw sorrow on every face.

"We love you, Psyche!" a voice called out.

Then came another and another. "We love you, Psyche! We love you!"

Eventually everyone called out softly, as if they were singers in a chorus, "We love you, Psyche! We love you."

Now, when it was too late, Psyche regretted having been closed to the love the people had offered.

The sad processional made its mournful way through the village, and there, on the other side, a heavy and dark silence covered them. Ahead was the forest path that would bring Psyche to the top of the mountain, where her husband waited.

Psyche stopped, then turned to her parents.

"You do not need to go up the mountain with me," she told them.

"But—"

"It is better if I go by myself."

"We don't want you to go up there alone," her mother interjected in a trembling voice.

"Thank you, Mother, but even if you were with me, I would still be alone. Each of us must meet our fate as if we no longer have a mother or father, brother or sister."

Psyche hugged and kissed her parents. Then, taking a torch from one of the soldiers, she started up the path.

The Walk Up the Mountain

Now that she was alone, the tears that had been waiting for release longer than Psyche knew sprang from her eyes and poured down her face.

Tears had been accumulating since Psyche had been in her mother's womb and heard her father whisper that she was going to be his little princess. Each of us has tears from the moment we are conceived. We need tears so we can express those sorrows for which there will never be words. But tears can speak the language that is unique to them only if we tell them they can. When Psyche's tears heard that she was going to be a princess, they knew it would be hard for them to be part of Psyche's life. There were so many things a princess could not do, like eat with her fingers, laugh too loudly, or speak above a quiet and measured tone. Last but by no means least, a princess could not cry. Woe be to those who do not care for their tears.

When Psyche fell and skinned a knee, her nurse would say, "You must not cry. You are a princess and the people of the kingdom need you to be strong."

If one of her sisters said something that hurt her feelings, and then with tears in her eyes, she told her parents, they would say, "If mere words bring tears to your eyes, what will you do when something truly awful happens? You are a princess, Psyche, and princesses don't cry."

On this particular night, as Psyche made her way slowly up the path to the mountaintop, no one was there to remind her that she was a princess. The only beings who saw her were the trees and the stones, and they saw a lonely and frightened young woman who was crying so hard they feared her grief would break *their* hearts.

Stones and trees have been the silent witnesses of grieving people and creatures since before Time started counting itself. They knew how to tend sorrow, but only if the person sat with his back against the trunk of a tree, or carried a Tear Keeper stone—but those were hard to find. Not able to relieve Psyche's sorrow, the trees and stones did what they could to ease her way; the trees raised low-hanging branches that stretched across the path, so they would not strike her in the face, while stones moved to the side if it seemed she was going to trip over one of them.

The release of tears was like cleansing a wound with a healing unguent, and the heaviness that had draped Psyche's life with Sorrow's cloak softly fell away.

Psyche's New Home

When Psyche reached the top of the mountain, the flame of her torch shrank back in fear of the dense darkness. The flame flickered, trembled, and died, though there was no wind. At the same instant, the torch flew from Psyche's hand as if someone or something had snatched it. She shrieked, expecting that something or someone would reach out of the darkness and take her. She held her breath and waited.

Moments passed. Nothing happened. Psyche looked around, though she could see only darkness. She listened for the sound of a presence, but heard nothing except the sound of her breathing and the beating of her heart.

Unable to see where she was, Psyche was afraid to move. For all she knew, she could be standing at the edge of a precipice, and one step might send her falling through space to her death. Carefully she dropped to her knees and felt the ground around her. Her fingers brushed against stone. Slowly she moved her hands upward against what seemed to be the rough contours of a large boulder. Psyche moved to sit with her back resting against it.

Time went by. It must have been many hours, because her fear eased and was replaced by impatience. Where was the monster? What was taking him so long? Or was he torturing her by making her wait? Finally, she fell into a deep sleep.

Night was about to flee from Day's onslaught when Psyche felt a soft and warm breeze. Suddenly, as if it had arms, the wind lifted her up.

"What's happening?" she wondered. She was flying, but how?

As if hearing her question, a soft but deep voice said, "I am Favonius, the West Wind. Your husband asked me to bring you to him, which it is my pleasure and honor to do. Would you like to feel for a few moments what it is like to be a bird?"

"Oh, yes!" Psyche exclaimed.

She relaxed into unseen arms, which held her tightly, and gave herself over to the joy of not being bound to the earth. Higher and higher West Wind took her. In the pale light of predawn Psyche could see the Great Blue Sea, delineating the southern border of the kingdom. To the north were the towering heights of the mountains. At the very edge of the eastern horizon was the Lost Kingdom, a place where only the ruins of an ancient and forgotten realm remained. To the west Psyche could make out the Kingdom of the Ferns, the beautiful place where her sisters now lived with their husbands.

Beneath her was the kingdom where until yesterday she had been a princess. She was surprised to see that there were still crowds of people along the road leading from the palace. Her father and mother walked among the people, something she could not recall her parents ever doing. But there they were, shaking hands and putting their arms around some who were crying.

"Your parents are consoling the people who are grieving your absence," Favonius explained.

Tears came to her eyes. "Can you take me down, just for a moment, so that they might see that I am well?"

"Pleasing you would be my delight, dear Psyche, but your husband gave me strict instructions to bring you to his realm."

"Then, if you cannot take me down so the people can see me one last time, tell me about my husband. Is he truly a monster?"

"There are those who would say so, and there are those who would say not. That is as much as I can say."

"Can, or will?" Psyche wanted to know.

"Can and will," Favonius responded. Then, as if to stop any further conversation, he did a series of somersaults, turning over and over, and Psyche squealed with delight.

Finally, Favonius began gliding earthward with the gentleness of floating dandelion fluff.

"That is where you spent the night," Favonius said.

Psyche turned her head to see a mountain, a huge boulder sitting at its edge. While there was a path leading up the summit on the other side, this side of the mountain was sheer stone that looked as slippery as ice. At the mountain's base was a swift-moving river bordered by a grove of trees so tall and thick Psyche thought they must have been growing since the creation of the world. Beyond the trees was a broad valley, and it was here Favonius brought Psyche and set her down gently in a meadow of grasses and wildflowers.

"I must leave you now," he said. "Your husband has asked me to be at your service. If you should ever need me, you need only say my name. One of my breezes will carry your voice to me, and I will come. You should rest now because tonight you will become a wife."

Psyche realized just how tired she was, lay down in the soft grasses, and was asleep at once.

Sun was feeling cranky that morning. He had tossed and turned all night, despairing because Psyche had been taken away. If there had ever been a morning when he did not want to get up, this was it. But he had a job to do, so he struggled out of bed and took a sleepy step onto the sky. With each step, he created the reds and oranges of dawn and, finally, the blues of the day.

Midway through the morning, as Sun struggled past the top of the mountain from which Favonius had taken Psyche, he looked down into the hidden valley.

"Psyche!" he shouted as he saw her asleep in the grass. Sun was so happy, he began shining brighter than he ever had. His light became so glaring and bright, people had to put their hands over their eyes, but even that did not help much.

In the Kingdom of the Ferns, one Alexander Agrippa Antony, an olive-oil taster, walked out his front door, and the sunlight was so strong, it knocked him down! Triple A, as he preferred to be called, picked himself up and hurried back inside. There were olive oils coming in that day from Sausalito, Spain, and Glendale, Greece, and he had a lot of sniffing to do. But if the sunlight knocked him down every time he left the house, he would never get to work, and inferior olive oil might be allowed into the kingdom. Triple A could not imagine anything more horrible than people cooking with inferior olive oil.

He had to do something, but what? Triple A thought and thought and thought, and then he snapped his fingers. He went to his cellar and found an old jar, caked with dirt inside. He put the jar in front of his eyes, then tied it around his head. When he went back out, he could see without being blinded by the sun's exuberant glare.

When people saw what Triple A had on his eyes, they asked him if he had more jars like that. He had a basement full because his wife, like mine, never threw anything out. He sold all the jars, and Triple A and his wife became wealthy people. In case you were wondering, that is how sunglasses were invented. However, even though Triple A no longer needed a job, he and his nose remained in the forefront of the war against bad olive oil!

Sun's warmth woke Psyche. Sitting up, she saw that she was in a grassy meadow of the softest greens. Red, blue, and yellow wildflowers glistened among the grasses like stars in the night sky. The air was warm, and Favonius had sent a breeze as delicate as rose petals to stroke her.

She stood up and stretched, giving a big yawn, wondering what she was supposed to do next. Should she wait where she was for her husband to come and get her? That was when she noticed a path leading into the tall trees of the forest.

"That must be the way to the home of my husband," she said to herself. Without hesitating, she started toward it, eager for what was to come. She was surprised that she was not afraid, but no monster she had ever heard of had the power to command West Wind to do its bidding. Plus, she was hungry. She had not eaten since yesterday. No. It had been the day before that. Yesterday she had been too busy being sad and worrying.

Psyche made her way across the meadow to the path and followed it into the woods, where it was cooler. In a short while she came to a small bridge undulating with light. Looking more closely, she saw it was made of long strands of silver as thin as hair. Beneath the bridge flowed a stream. Its sound was not that of water going from its source to the sea. Instead, it sang a beautiful melody, and the words it sang surprised her:

> Beautiful Psyche, be my bride,
> O gods be praised.
> Psyche has come to be at my side,
> O gods be praised.

"Welcome to your home, my lady," came the soft voice of a woman.

"Who said that?" Psyche wanted to know, looking around but seeing no one.

"I am Cinxia, the goddess of marriage. Your husband asked me to come and make sure all of his preparations for you are to your liking," the voice answered. "Please continue across the bridge. You are not far from your home now."

Psyche looked around once more, but again saw no one. Cautiously she stepped onto the bridge and was amazed that something which looked so delicate was, at the same time, very strong. When she reached the other side, she saw a path and followed it until she came to a clearing. In its center stood a high wall, but instead of being constructed from blocks of stone, it was made of colors—sky blues, ocean blues, violet and iris blues, turquoise, sapphire, lavender and wisteria blues. Psyche went closer and put out her hands to touch the wall. To her surprise, it was as hard as the marble floors of her father's palace.

"I don't understand," Psyche said quietly.

Cinxia said, "Every day the blues of the sky are created anew by Sun as he rises. Each evening as Sun leaves the heavens, he takes blue colors to prevent Night from devouring all of them. At your husband's request, Sun gave him some of the leftover blues to use in building this palace."

What man was so powerful that he could make a request of Sun and have it granted? And how did he make a solid wall from leftover pieces of the sky? Only a god could do something as marvelous as that. But Apollo had said her husband was a monster, not a god. Could someone be a monster and yet create beauty?

"Come, my lady," the voice interrupted her thoughts.

No sooner were the words said than a door opened in the wall where Psyche would have sworn none existed. She walked inside and found herself on the grounds of a palace.

At the center was a round fountain of wrought gold bubbling with a liquid the colors of strawberries, raspberries, and plums, but unlike every other fountain Psyche had seen, this one made music as if it were a lyre being played by Apollo. At the base of the fountain, planted in a series of concentric circles, were flowers larger than any she had ever seen and in colors for which there were no names. Small birds flitted among the flowers like wisps of wind playing with each other.

At the far end of the grounds stood a palace, a long building in the shape of an arrow, though Psyche could not see the pointed tip. The building was deep red in color because it was built from unfulfilled desires and passions, emotions as strong as iron and brick, which could last for eternity.

As Psyche approached the building, the doors opened of themselves, revealing a long hallway gleaming with light. Psyche walked in and looked around. On both walls were paintings of beautiful women and men in poses of love. The floor was a mosaic of a serpent, made of sapphires, rubies, and emeralds, which extended the length of the hallway. The ceiling was covered with gold leaf.

"Please," came the invisible voice of Cinxia, "explore your new home. Anything that is not to your liking will be taken care of immediately."

Slowly and timidly, Psyche went through the palace, peering into every room. Each had walls of gold shining so brightly, it was as if each had its own sun. Etched into the golden walls were more drawings of people in poses of love. At the center of each room was a long table, and each table was piled almost ceiling high with jeweled bracelets, necklaces, and rings, and gowns of silk stitched with golden threads.

Even though she was a princess and had been around wealth all of her life, such riches as she saw in the palace's ten rooms were beyond her imagination and comprehension. How had one man amassed a wealth greater than numbers by which to count it?

At the end of the corridor was the largest room of all. Here the walls were covered with cloth made of golden threads. At one end of the room was a table with a marble top. On it lay a mirror set inside a gold frame with a golden handle. Next to the mirror were jars of lotions and small bowls of colored powders for makeup. At the other end of the room was a large bed with sheets so soft, Psyche thought they had to have been made from clouds. Laid across the bed were silken gowns shimmering with subtle hues of red, green, brown, and yellow. At the foot of the bed was a large chest overflowing with bracelets, necklaces, rings, and tiaras studded with every kind of jewel the earth had to offer.

"All the treasures you see, my lady, are gifts from your husband," Cinxia said.

"When do I get to meet my-my husband?" Psyche wanted to know. "Do you know him? What is he like?"

"It is not for me to say anything about him. Just know that this is where he will come to you tonight. Why don't you rest? When you awake, your servants will have your bath ready. After you dress, you will come to the Great Hall for your wedding banquet."

Psyche lay down on the bed, which was as soft as the moment when two people realize they love each other. Almost immediately, she was asleep.

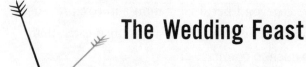

The Wedding Feast

It was evening when Psyche awoke.

"Your bath awaits you, my lady," came Cinxia's now familiar voice.

Across the hallway was a room with walls covered in marble and a floor made of wood from the tall cedars of Lebanon. At the center was a large rectangular pool filled with hot water from which vapors rose.

Invisible hands undressed Psyche, then escorted her into the pool. She lay back and closed her eyes. The water warmed not only her body but, as if it had hands, it smoothed away her lingering fears and anxieties. She could not believe that harm could come to her in a place of such beauty.

When she came out of the pool, the invisible ones were waiting with a large towel to dry her. They anointed her body with oil, then dressed her in a gown of white silk.

Psyche could not remember ever feeling so cared for. Was this what it was like to feel loved? Whoever her husband was, it seemed he wanted nothing of her except her pleasure.

The invisible hands guided her toward the Great Hall where a long table stood. Psyche sat down and immediately a goblet of wine shimmering with the reds of sunset appeared before her eyes and settled gently on the table next to her right hand. Smiling, she sipped. Although her father had the finest wine cellar in the kingdom, no wine in it came close to the complex flavors of this one.

Dishes of fruit, greens, soups, and meats floated through the air and silently alit on the table. As she started to eat, a melody of exquisite sweetness came from an invisible lyre. It was joined by a chorus of voices. Still, Psyche saw no one.

When she finished eating, the dishes vanished as mysteriously as they had arrived. The music stopped.

"Thank you," Psyche said.

"It is an honor to serve you who are about to become a bride," returned the familiar voice. "Is there anything else you desire?"

"No. Thank you."

Psyche returned to her bedroom, feeling alive in every part of her body. Now, for the first time in her life, she understood: eating began not with putting food into one's mouth but with the eyes luxuriating in the many reds in one goblet of wine, with the shades of green in just one salad leaf. Eating included the aromas that rose from the food. Eating was chewing slowly in order not only to taste but to know the textures of greens, bread, meat, and vegetables.

Psyche took off her gown, pulled the sheet over her warm and expectant body, and waited eagerly for her husband's arrival. Though the god Apollo was incapable of telling an untruth, she could no longer believe that the man coming to her that night was a monster. Or if he was, perhaps every man should be a monster like him.

Psyche's Husband

You might be wondering where Cupid was while all this was going on. Well, he was seeing to every detail— checking the temperature of the water in Psyche's bath; in the basement, deciding on the bottle of wine; in the kitchen, overseeing the cooking. He wanted everything to be perfect for Psyche, which was why he had gotten Cinxia involved, though not without paying a price. She had made him promise that he would stop shooting lead-tipped arrows into the husband or wife in a happy marriage. He readily agreed, shuddering to think how he would feel if someone should turn Psyche against him. He even felt bad for all the good marriages he had broken up.

Cinxia had been happy to assist Cupid. Although he was the god of love, he knew nothing about marriage. There was so much she wanted to tell him, but there was not time, and he would not have listened. She was aware that mortals, and even gods, thought love was a feeling, but feelings could come and go like rain. Love was a choice one made each day, regardless of how one was feeling toward or about the beloved. Perhaps Cupid would learn that in time. He thought he was choosing Psyche, but he was being chosen by an emotion that was more lust than love. However, her part in the love story of Cupid and Psyche was finished for the time being. What happened next was up to Cupid.

"Thank you for everything," Cupid said to her as she prepared to go. They were sitting on a stone bench in the palace garden.

"It was my pleasure. I have trained the spirits who remain in everything they should do, not that they needed much training."

"If I might ask, who are they?"

Cinxia smiled sadly. "They are the spirits of those who married and their partner died before the marriage reached its fulfillment. Now, I must return to Olympus. Perhaps I will have the opportunity to attend a more formal and proper wedding between you and Psyche in our celestial realm?"

"Of course," Cupid responded, knowing that the only way he could marry Psyche on Olympus was over his mother's dead body—and Venus could not die.

Cinxia went to her waiting chariot, which was pulled by two phoenixes, and she was off.

Cupid was alone now. The moment he had been waiting for, the moment to go to Psyche and make her his wife, had arrived. And he was afraid.

As far as I'm concerned, he should have been. Now, I'm not bragging or anything like that, but it has been my privilege to—how shall I say this?—to know, in the Biblical sense, more than one woman over the course of my long life. Knowing someone else is not easy. To truly know another, you have to open yourself to being known. For me, at least, this embrace of the soul through the medium of the body was and is terrifying. I've been with my present wife fifteen years, and I'm learning that the act of knowing and being known is not something that happens once. It must happen repeatedly if the love is going to expand throughout the course of her life and mine.

Cupid did not know any of that. All he knew was that he was afraid. What if he went to Psyche and she didn't like him? What if she took one look at him and found him unattractive? What if she didn't like the way he kissed?

Suddenly he stopped what he was thinking and feeling. Had he lost his mind? Why was he, the god of love, caring about a mortal's opinion of him?

He was acting like a mortal who had been pierced by one of his gold-tipped arrows. How did they tolerate the constant yearning for the other? How did they withstand the overwhelming desire to merge themselves with the other and become one being?

Cupid was disgusted with himself. He hated that Psyche was so important to him, hated that he would do almost anything to put a smile on her face, and most of all, he hated feeling that he was incomplete without her.

He still did not want to think about what his mother would do when she found out how completely he had disobeyed and deceived her. Her fear of his arrows would keep her from doing anything to him directly. Instead she would unleash her wrath on Psyche. But anything Venus did to Psyche would be as if she were doing it to him.

"Love *is* madness!" he exclaimed, angry now. He wanted to apologize to every person he had ever shot with a gold-tipped arrow. He had not known he was infecting mortals with helplessness, with a loss of will and control, with a loss of self. Love had put him in a state where he was no longer who he had been but had no idea who he would become. That depended on Psyche.

"I am Cupid and I will not have it!" he declared. "I will

send a breeze to Favonius and have him come and return her to her parents and let her meet whatever fate waits her there. Perhaps I wrongly interpreted Apollo's words. Perhaps there is truly a monster waiting to marry her, and I took her away before the monster could claim her. Better she be with a monster than remain here and turn my life into chaos."

Cupid got up. Then he stopped. He looked toward the far end of the palace where Psyche's room was. He imagined her lying on the bed awaiting him. He stood for a long while, staring. Finally he said, "It will do no harm if I look at her one last time before Favonius returns her to where she belongs."

He flew to the balcony outside her room. The double doors opened of themselves. Cupid walked silently into the room. Moon, as if obeying orders, shone her light directly on Psyche.

He was startled by a hesitant shyness that made him afraid to go closer to her. He who had been so bold as to shoot a gold-tipped arrow into a god as great as Apollo was suddenly afraid to utter a word, or even breathe loudly in the presence of such beauty.

Cupid stood transfixed. Looking at Psyche, a softness came over his face, and gentleness suffused his body. He was filled with a tender yearning. The mere sight of her promised satisfaction of a hunger he had not known he had until he saw her that first time.

Her oval face was shaped like the heart beating so rapidly in his chest. Long, dark hair framed the face and softened it. Though her eyes were closed, he thought he could see the dark eyes beneath the closed lids. Her lips were relaxed and slightly parted, as if waiting for his lips. Psyche was more beautiful than he had remembered, more beautiful than anyone had the right to be. He wanted to be—*had* to be—a part of that beauty.

You, dear reader, and I know that Cupid's eyes did not stop at her face. Cupid may have been a god, but he was a *male* god, and many men, your storyteller included, like to look at women's faces *and* bodies, and not necessarily in that order.

The sheet beneath which Psyche lay clung to her body like it had been made exclusively for her to wear as a garment, because it outlined the slope of her breasts and curves of her body. Cupid gasped as he imagined himself pulling back the sheet and gazing on the full beauty of the body hidden beneath it. He wanted her more than he had ever wanted anything in his eternal life.

There are many, men and women, who say such male attention to women's bodies is sexist. This is true, but it is also true that there is an undeniable beauty to the female form, which has entranced men and women for at least as long as humans have made visual records of their lives. Women's fashions are designed to enhance the beauty of the female form, to draw the attention of men and women to that form. All of us, men and women, do everything we know to make ourselves attractive.

So Cupid should not be faulted for staring so hungrily at Psyche. More than sexual feelings were aroused in him as he gazed on her. Some of you may think I am trying to rationalize and justify lust. That is not so. I do not think I am alone in experiencing sexual desire and transcendent ecstasy as two halves of a godly wholeness, a wholeness we call beauty.

Whether it is physical or spiritual (and I'm not sure the two should be separated), beauty takes us out of our narrow self-centeredness. In beauty we experience ourselves as part of and belonging to something larger and greater than what is encompassed by our "I." When we are penetrated by beauty, human or divine, we become transcendent. And that is so, even if the one being penetrated is a god.

Cupid still could not move, which is not an uncommon response in the presence of beauty. Even gods and goddesses are not exempt from beauty's forbidding and terrifying power. Let there be no mistake: Cupid was afraid. Perhaps more than any of the deities on Olympus, he was the one always in control of himself. Let the other deities entrap themselves in human emotions, but he knew better. And so it was until he saw Psyche.

Now standing there, looking at her, for the first time in his eternal life Cupid faced a choice: maintain control and leave Psyche, or submit to his desire for her and never be wholly in control of his life ever again. (And for him, *ever* was not a figure of speech.)

There come moments in each of our journeys when we

can no longer continue our lives as they are. But neither can we see what we will become. We either go forward, with no idea of where we are going or what we are doing, or we remain as we are—and begin to die, though we do not realize that is the choice we have made. This is why love is such a fearful undertaking, and why, for so many women especially, the wedding day is fraught with terror and tears. Why do people voluntarily agree to relinquish a degree of control over their lives and pledge themselves to take into consideration the needs, desires, and shortcomings of another for the rest of their lives?

Cupid had no answer, except the certain knowledge that a life without Psyche's beauty was not a life he wanted.

Trembling inside, he crossed the room and sat down on the edge of the bed. Leaning over, he kissed her softly on the cheek. Psyche's eyes opened, but as if obeying a command, clouds moved in front of the moon, plunging the room into darkness so that Psyche could not see.

"Who—," she started to say, but Cupid placed a finger on her lips, silencing her. Then his arms reached down to cradle her head, and as he brought her up to meet his lips, the sheet slid from her. As her arms encircled his neck and his encircled hers, their bodies met.

It occurs to me to wonder: was this the first time Cupid made love? I think so. How odd that the god of love had never made love until this night. Was he nervous? Did he perspire with anxiety? Was his heart beating with fear? All that and more.

The making of love is not simple. To make love, we *touch* the body of another but we *grasp* that which cannot be seen—the strands of desire, fear, anxiety, pleasure, and beauty—and with that person, we braid these emotions so that two become one and the boundary dissolves between where you end and the other begins, and you and the other become a single being.

So it was with Cupid and with Psyche that night.

So it was.

Psyche's Loneliness

Love requires close and careful attention by each to the other. You would think that Cupid, the god of love, would have known this. Apparently he did not.

Each night he came to Psyche and they made exquisite love. However, after a while, that was not enough for Psyche. She wanted to know who came to her in the night and made her feel more alive than she had known was possible. She wanted to make love in all the ways, and not just with their bodies.

"What is your name?" she asked Cupid one night.

"Why do you need to know my name when you possess my soul?"

"If I cannot know your name, may I light a lamp so I can see your face?"

"If you should ever see my face, you will lose me forever."

"Why?" Psyche wanted to know. "Are you ugly? Are you afraid I won't love you if I see your face?"

"Perhaps I am afraid that if you see my face, it will be *that* that you will love and not me."

"I understand, believe me. I know what that feels like."

"Perhaps you do. Nonetheless, if you see my face, I will leave you."

"Then, tell me your name."

"Call me your beloved. That is the name I know myself by since you came into my life."

"I could love you even more if I knew who you are, if I could gaze upon your face."

Cupid did not know that one way of making love is to share your fears with the other. His situation was like that of a wealthy and beautiful woman who is afraid a man will love her only for her beauty and money and not for herself. Cupid wanted to be loved for himself and not because he was a god. He was afraid that if Psyche knew his true identity, the quality of her love might change and she would regard him as a possession to be displayed like a rare vase or sculpture. Of course Psyche knew even better than he did how it felt to be regarded as an object.

But Cupid could not think about very much beyond the pleasure that holding and touching her gave him. He was satisfying his physical need and desire, but he was not yet making love. Love is not made if you are unwilling to risk being seen for who you are.

His refusal to reveal himself to Psyche nagged at her during the long days when she was alone. Despite being surrounded by wealth, despite having servants, invisible ones, who waited on her throughout the day, Psyche began to feel she was living in a prison. What good was it to be surrounded by wealth and beauty if she had no one with whom to share it?

Cupid spent his days feeling the pain of her absence. There were many times each day when he had to hold himself back from rushing to the palace and taking her in his arms. His days were as empty as hers, but while his hours were filled with longing for her, hers became more and more filled with loneliness and resentment. When resentment is added to loneliness, the result is a quiet anger. That spells trouble in any relationship.

The Sisters

Thomasina and Calla were as different from Psyche as hard is from soft. Psyche had grown up wondering what beauty was and if she had a responsibility to it. Thomasina and Calla had grown up thinking that their one task in life was the maintenance of their beauty. That's a lot of work. I know, not because I am beautiful but because I subscribe to five women's fashion magazines, all of which document that being beautiful takes a lot of time and a lot of work throughout the day, all day, and every day. Well, imagine how hard it was to stay beautiful back in Thomasina's and Calla's day, when there were no magazines to tell them what to put on where, and what not to put on there, and why.

Each morning after Psyche's sisters had sunshine brushed into their hair, they had to decide which gowns to wear that day, because they couldn't wear in the afternoon what they had worn in the morning, and—Juno forbid—they certainly couldn't wear in the evening what they had worn in the afternoon or in the morning. Then they had to decide what shoes and jewelry to wear with each gown, and having decided all that, they would change their minds and start all over. Eventually they would settle on what gown to wear and what accessories went with what. Then it was time to put on makeup. That is far too complicated a subject for my male brain. As far as I am concerned, the color red is red. But when my daughter was fourteen, she knew there was plum red, sunrise red, sunset red, autumn red, winter red, spring red, and that was just nail polish. There were a whole bunch of other reds for the lips, and still more reds for the cheeks. It took months of experimentation and practice before a woman understood which red looked best at what time of day and in what season of the year and with what garments. Any man who thinks men are smarter than women needs to have his manhood examined.

Which brings me to the men who married Thomasina

and Calla. The story did not give them anything to say, which is why the story did not give them names. But I don't like people wandering around in a story without names, so I'm going to call them Dumb and Dumber.

The only reason they wanted to marry Thomasina and Calla was because they were good to look at. So is chocolate cake, but nobody has ever married one (though there are women I know who if given a choice between a lifetime supply of good chocolate and their husbands would not think twice about telling their husbands to start packing). Dumb and Dumber couldn't think of anything else but how admired they would be for having such beautiful wives. If Dumb and Dumber had come and talked to me, I would have set them straight. A long time ago, between marriages number one and number two—or maybe it was during marriage number four. Well, whenever it was—I had a girlfriend who was *glamourlicious*. Every man who saw us together envied me. (I don't think women envied her for being with me, but that's neither here nor there.) For about a month, I enjoyed thinking about all the men who wished they were me. But after that, I was hoping one of them would come and take my place. My girlfriend was not interested in talking about anything except how beautiful she looked in this dress and that dress, and did this dress complement her eye color, and did that dress make her look fat? Being married to a glamourlicious woman was tiring.

If Dumb and Dumber had talked to me, I would have

also told them that one of the biggest problems in a marriage is what you expect of the other and what the other expects of you. The closer each person's expectations come to meeting and shaking hands with each other, the better the marriage is going to be. Unfortunately, Thomasina and Calla and Dumb and Dumber had expectations of each other as different as rocks and water.

Thomasina and Calla expected they would be living in palaces at least as large as the one in which they had grown up, have servants who would do whatever they asked, and that they would devote each day to making themselves beautiful. But when Thomasina and Calla arrived at their respective homes, they knew immediately that they and their husbands were living in different marriages.

Dumb and Dumber lived in large houses, but they were not palaces with paintings of the gods and goddesses on the walls, and gardens in which the shrubbery had been cultivated to look like unicorns and griffins. (And please don't interrupt the story and ask me what a griffin is. To tell the truth, I don't know; but it would not change the story one bit if I did know, so what does it matter?) Thomasina and Calla might have been able to adjust to the fact that their husbands did not live in palaces, but there was another and much bigger problem.

Dumb and Dumber each had only two servants, a man who served them and an old woman who did a poor job of cooking and cleaning. This meant that Thomasina and Calla would have to tend to the mending, washing, and ironing of their many clothes, to mix and prepare their many rouges, powders, and perfumes, as well as to heat and pour the water they required for their many baths each day. And, Juno forbid, they would have to brush their own hair. Well, when they understood the situation, they fainted dead away.

The two sisters lived miles apart, but each knew immediately what had to be done and they did it without hesitating. They sent word to their father of their predicament. The king sent back eight servant girls, four for each daughter. And he also sent word that their younger sister had been taken by a monster. They could not have cared less about what happened to Psyche, but they also knew this: when opportunity knocks, you better open the door. They now had a good excuse to get away from their husbands and go home to be treated like they deserved. So, pretending anguish and concern for their baby sister, Thomasina and Calla took their servants and returned to the palace.

They had expected their return to be met with joy by their parents. But the king and queen were dressed in sackcloth, and mourning what they imagined Psyche's fate to have been. They scarcely noticed that their two older daughters had returned.

High on the list of things that Thomasina and Calla disliked was being ignored. Very quickly they realized there was only one way to get their parents' attention. They did not want to do it, but if they were going to be the center of attention, they had no choice.

"We will go to the mountain where Psyche was to meet the monster, and see if we can learn her fate," Calla announced to the king and queen.

"I've already lost one daughter," the king said. "I don't want to lose the two I have left."

"Don't worry, Father. We will be all right," Thomasina assured him. "Hopefully, when we return, we will have news of Psyche, perhaps good news." Calla looked at Thomasina in amazement at the ease with which Thomasina lied. If Calla had not known better, she would have believed that Thomasina actually cared about Psyche.

The king's mood brightened at the possibility that Psyche might yet live. And off the sisters went, disgusted with their father for his (mistaken as far as they were concerned) love for Psyche, but delighted to be away from their husbands, whom they hoped never to see again.

Cupid Warns Psyche

It was Auster, South Wind, who brought word to Cupid about the sisters. Well, to give credit where credit is due, it was the trees who told South Wind.

Trees know practically everything that goes on. Their leaves are like ears, and with that many ears, there is not much they don't hear. They might stand there looking dumb, but trees are smart. Not only do they hear words, they can also hear thoughts. The trees knew that the sisters did not care about Psyche and that if they found her alive, they would kill her.

When South Wind blew through the trees, they told him everything they had heard. That's what's going on any time you see the wind shaking trees. The wind is collecting all the news the trees have learned that day. Then the wind spreads what it has learned to whoever needs to know. So, the next time a wind is blowing in your face, listen. The wind is trying to tell you something.

Cupid had no problem understanding what Auster told him, and that night he warned Psyche.

"My love, something may happen which will seek to destroy our relationship," he told her.

"What are you referring to?" Psyche wanted to know.

"It is your sisters. To win the affection of your parents, they are pretending to be distressed by what they believe to have been your death. Soon they will come to the top of the mountain from whence West Wind brought you here, to see if they can discover your fate. They will call out your name and you will hear them. I warn you: do not answer them. I will be deeply hurt if you do, and you will lose all you have now."

"Beloved, I would sooner die than do something that would hurt you."

But words uttered in darkness can lose much of their conviction when scrutinized in the light of day. Psyche had never been close to her sisters, nor they to her. If asked, Psyche would have said they hated her. But now that

Thomasina and Calla were coming to look for her, Psyche chose to ignore what she knew about them. And the thought of seeing her sisters made her even more aware of how lonely she was.

All that day Psyche cried. Her tears were not only from loneliness, however. These were also the tears of anger and resentment. How dare her husband, whoever he was, refuse to let her see her sisters. How dare he not allow her to, at the very least, take away their anguish by letting them know she was alive. How dare he!

Cupid heard her tears and came as soon as Night covered the sky. He held her in his arms, but her sobbing did not stop. Cupid may have been a god, but, in one respect, he was like practically all men: he could not withstand a woman's tears.

"Beloved Psyche. You promised me one thing, but you have spent the day regretting that promise. You are angry with me because you think I am denying you something you need. I assure you I am not. I seek only to save you from yourself and to save us. Alas, I see that it is not in my power. Do what you think best. But I warn you. When you realize the damage you have done, it will be too late to repair it."

If Psyche had stopped to ask how he knew about her sisters, how he knew she had cried all day, she would have understood that only a god could have such knowledge. But she was incapable of knowing anything except her overwhelming loneliness.

"Please understand," she began, "it would do my heart

so much good to see my sisters. They grieve for me and I need to let them know that not only am I alive, but that I am married. Would you mind if I gave them a few pieces of jewelry? I have more than I can ever wear. Please, my love." And she began to cry again.

"Do as you think best," Cupid responded. "But listen to me. Your sisters have minds that care only for evil. They will do everything they can to convince you to see what I look like. I repeat: if you look at me, all the happiness you have now will vanish."

"I understand," Psyche told him in all sincerity. "I would not do anything that would hurt our love. Even being held and kissed by Cupid himself could not fill me with the joy I find in your arms."

For an instant, Cupid was tempted to light the oil lamp and let her see from whose embrace and kisses came the joy she spoke of. But a sadness overcame him as he realized that Psyche would have said anything at that moment to get her way.

"I will command West Wind to bring your sisters here. You should pray that the gods will have mercy on your soul."

The Sisters Visit

The next morning, Psyche had just finished breakfast when she heard two voices calling her name. "Psyche! Psyche!"

"My sisters!" she exclaimed. "My sisters are calling for me!"

Psyche called for West Wind. When he arrived, she instructed him to go to the mountain and bring the two women calling her name.

Psyche was waiting outside the palace when Favonius sat Thomasina and Calla down. She ran to greet them, giving both many hugs and kisses.

Thomasina and Calla were too busy looking at the garden and the palace to notice Psyche's demonstrations of affection.

"I am so happy to see you," Psyche told them. "Come in and let me show you my new home."

As the two sisters followed Psyche from room to room, their mouths opened wider and wider in disbelief at the wealth they saw. And if that were not enough, there were the invisible servants who prepared baths for them and, later, served them a sumptuous meal, which, they noticed, Psyche had done nothing to prepare.

Psyche saw that her sisters were not eating and wanted to know what was wrong. "If the food is not to your liking, please tell me, and I will have another meal prepared."

"Everything is fine," Thomasina said. She and Calla smiled tightly.

"You are so fortunate to have married a man of such wealth," Thomasina continued. "Poor Calla and I married nobility, but, alas, what good is a man who has a full title and an empty purse?"

"What does your husband do?" Calla wanted to know. "He must be a very important person to have a palace like this and riches unlike any we've ever seen. What did you say his name was?"

"I didn't say," Psyche answered, a little flustered.

"Where is he? We would love to meet him," Thomasina put in.

"He . . . he . . . yes, he went hunting. That's what he spends all his time doing. I seldom see him myself." She gave a smile. "Oh, dear. Look. It is growing dark. How fast the time went by. Come. Would you like to take some jewels with you?"

Thomasina and Calla started drooling at the mouth. Psyche got up from the table, and her sisters followed as she led them down the corridor into a room where the table was piled high with diamonds, rubies, emeralds, and jewels no one had gotten around to giving names to. Thomasina and Calla filled their pockets, then stuffed their bras with so many jewels, they could hardly move.

Psyche hurried them out of the house, nervous that they might ask her more questions about her husband. When outside, Psyche called for West Wind, who was resting atop a tree.

"Take them back to where you found them, friend Wind."

As Favonius lifted Thomasina and Calla into the air, he thought they were heavier than when he had brought them. He understood as he listened to them talk.

"It's not fair!" Thomasina declared.

"You can say that again!" exclaimed Calla. "Invisible servants who wait on her hand and foot."

"Plates and goblets of gold! Room after room filled with jewels and fine garments."

"Why is she the one who always gets everything?"

"Father loved her more than he did us. And now, she has what must be the wealthiest man in the world for a husband."

"It's not right!"

"No, it isn't!"

Not only the jewels, but jealousy and malice, had made the two sisters so heavy that Favonius was tired and out of breath when he deposited them back on the mountaintop. Even though he was supposed to do whatever Cupid or Psyche wanted him to, he didn't know how many more trips he could make with those two. If they kept feeding each other's malice, they would end up as heavy as the mountain.

Thomasina and Calla were eager to get back to their parents' palace and look at the jewels they had acquired. However, if they returned with expressions of sated lust, everyone would be suspicious. So the two sisters tore each other's clothes and scratched their faces to make it appear that they were grieving for their "dead sister." They agreed not to tell their parents that Psyche was alive, for if they knew how well her marriage had turned out, they would love her even more.

When Thomasina and Calla reached the palace, they didn't have to say anything. Their disheveled appearance was enough to confirm the king's and queen's worst fears. Psyche was indeed dead! As their parents began weeping anew, the two sisters went up to their chambers and unburdened themselves of all the jewels they had taken, then hid them behind loose bricks in the fireplace. Then they began plotting: how could they kill Psyche and get her husband? Or at least his wealth.

Cupid Warns Psyche Again

Cupid was afraid. Psyche was naïve and had seen nothing of the sisters' animosity toward her. He had to find a way to convince her not to listen to them, not even to see them. If he didn't, Psyche would unwittingly destroy their relationship, and he did not know what he would do without her.

That night, in the darkness of the bedchamber, he told her again, "My love, you are in great danger."

"What do you mean?" she asked.

"Thomasina and Calla want to destroy you."

"Me?" she laughed nervously. "They are my sisters. They would not do anything to hurt me."

"Please listen to me. They are going to try to persuade you to look at my face. You must not. Indeed, if they try to visit you again, please do not let them come here."

"That would hurt their feelings. Please don't ask that of me."

"Very well. But you must not answer any of their questions about me. Do you understand?"

"No. My sisters are as curious about you as I am. Why won't you tell me who you are? Why won't you let me see your face?"

"You do not need to see my face to love me."

"No, but I would love you even more if I could see your face."

"But what if you saw my face and loved me less?"

"That would not be possible."

"How can you be sure?"

Psyche realized that she couldn't. She would have liked to think that she would still love him, but she could not say with certainty that she would have, and that made her feel ashamed.

"One more thing I need to tell you before I go," Cupid said, interrupting her thoughts. "You are carrying my child."

"What?" she exclaimed in joy and disbelief. "How do you know? I don't feel anything."

"I know much. For now, all you need to know is this: if you are able to resist your sisters when they implore you to look at my face, our child will be born divine. But if you disobey me, our child will be mortal. Do you understand?"

"Yes. Yes, I do," she responded eagerly, but she answered too quickly and with exaggerated emotion. "I don't think you trust me," she continued, tears in her voice. "When my sisters were here, did I betray you in any way?"

Reluctantly, Cupid admitted that she had not.

"You act as if I do not know how to take care of myself. I do. That is not the problem. You, my love, do not understand how terribly lonely I get during the day. You do not know how slowly the day crawls past as I sit and wait for your return. When my sisters visit, it helps time go faster. The minutes when I will be with you again are not as far apart when my sisters come and distract me from thinking of you.

"I promise that if you let me see them again, I will never again be curious to see what you look like."

With great reluctance Cupid agreed, but as he flew away that night, it was with tears in his eyes. He knew. All was lost.

The Sisters Return

Sun had scarcely begun his journey when Thomasina suddenly awoke. She knew how to get rid of Psyche and take all the riches for herself and Calla.

She woke her sister and shared the plan with her. Calla was ecstatic. The two sisters embraced, then dressed hurriedly and were on their way to the mountain.

When they arrived, they called out Psyche's name. She heard, then sent Favonius to bring them. Carrying two people of such evil was not to West Wind's liking, but he did so. When he set them down at the palace door, he hoped that when he took them back it would be the last time he had anything to do with them.

The two sisters rushed into the palace, shouting, "Psyche! Psyche! Are you all right? Sister! Where are you?"

When Psyche heard their voices, she came running. "Oh, sisters! I am so happy to see you!"

Thomasina was shrewd. She was content to spend the day chatting with Psyche about their childhoods and other inconsequential matters. If anyone had seen the sisters as they lay beside the pool and chatted after bathing, he would have thought no sisters had ever loved each other as much as these three.

Supper that evening was quite sumptuous, with course following course of melon balls, lobster tail, lamb in mustard sauce, perfumed rice, and wild peas in a lemon butter sauce. All of this was accompanied by the finest wines, and the meal was completed with fresh, ripe strawberries dipped in chocolate.

All three sisters looked like they were in a drunken stupor from the rich food, wine, and dessert. Thomasina and Calla had not, however, eaten as much as Psyche. They were as alert as deer ready to run at the snap of a twig. Thomasina and Calla exchanged looks: now was the time.

"Little sister," Thomasina began softly, "tell us again about your husband. I know you mentioned him last time, but I can't remember what you said."

Psyche was so groggy from all she had eaten and drunk that she could not remember what she had told them. "He's . . . he's . . . a, well, a merchant! He must travel a lot, of course, which is why he is not here to meet you."

Thomasina and Calla looked at each other again. Last time Psyche had said her husband was away hunting.

Calla reached over and took Psyche's hand, squeezing it softly. "Oh, poor Psyche!"

Psyche looked concerned. "Why do you pity me, Sister?"

"We know the truth, and we are disappointed that you would not confide in us, your sisters who love you so much."

"I-I-I have no secrets to hide," Psyche said, unconvincingly.

Now it was Thomasina's turn. "We are hurt that you mistrust us so."

"I don't know what you're talking about."

"When we were here before, you told us your husband was away hunting. Now you tell us he is a merchant."

"He . . . he is both," Psyche responded weakly, and then she started to cry. "Oh, dear sisters! Forgive me! I did not mean to lie to you. It is just that—" She stopped as she remembered what her husband had made her promise. But at that moment, he seemed so far away, she wondered if he were actually real.

"Go on," Calla said softly.

"I do not know what my husband does. And worst of all, I have never seen his face."

"How could that be?" they both asked.

"He comes at night, makes love to me in the dark, and leaves before the sun comes up."

Thomasina sighed deeply. "It is just as we feared."

"What did you fear?" Psyche asked eagerly.

"When father told us that the god Apollo said you were to be married to a monster, we asked Father to tell us more about this monster. He could not. He said he had been so devastated by what Apollo had told him, he had not wanted to know more. We upbraided him for not protecting you."

"Early this morning," Calla continued, "Thomasina and I went to Apollo's temple ourselves and asked him to describe this monster you married." She stopped.

"Please go on," Psyche pleaded.

The two sisters sighed dramatically.

"What Apollo told us was so awful I am reluctant to repeat it," Thomasina said. "After all, look at you. You live in the finest palace in all the world, with more wealth than you will ever know what to do with. You have invisible servants to carry out your every command. You eat the finest foods. Would that our husbands provided for us half as well. If our husbands did for us as yours does for you, we would not care what they looked like."

Psyche burst into tears. "Sister. Why do you torture me?

If you know something, it is cruel not to tell me. I have spent so much time trying to imagine what my husband looks like. Please. What did Apollo say to you?"

Thomasina looked at Calla. "Should we say what we learned?"

Calla hesitated. "I don't know. Our sister is delicate. I would not want to be responsible if we spoke and her heart was so startled by our news that it ceased beating."

"Stop it!" Psyche screamed, beyond herself with fear now. "Tell me this moment, or I shall call West Wind to remove you and keep you from coming here ever again."

"Very well," Thomasina said. "But we warned you." She paused, then went on. "Your husband comes to you in the guise of a man, but he is really an enormous snake with large jaws. He has a body that could wrap itself totally around you from head to foot. Worst of all, he has a bulging neck filled with poison."

"Oh no!" Psyche cried.

"I fear there is worse."

"What could be worse than what you have said already?"

"Only this. Your husband pampers you now. He will continue to do so as long as you do not bear him a child."

"Why? What will happen?"

"His favorite delicacy is a woman near the end of her pregnancy."

Psyche shrieked. "Oh no! No! No!"

"What's wrong?" Calla asked.

"He just told me that I-I am carrying his child."

"But how could he know?"

Psyche, weeping, shook her head. "I don't know. I don't know."

Thomasina couldn't believe what she was hearing. This was working out better than she could have dreamed.

Psyche, tears flowing down her face, hugged her sisters. "Thank you for telling me the truth, but now I am confused and frightened. Please tell me what to do."

Calla answered. "The moment Thomasina and I left Apollo's shrine, we began talking about that. We agreed that there is only one solution. Get the sharpest carving knife you have. Hide it in your bed. Tonight, after the monster makes love to you and falls asleep, light the lamp. Then take the knife and cut off his head. And do not be afraid. Thomasina and I will be close by, and when you have done the deed, we will hurry in and help you get away with all your treasures."

With tears still pouring down her face, Psyche nodded. "Thank you, Sisters! I do not know what I would have done without you."

Slowly, Psyche walked away.

When Thomasina and Calla heard Psyche close the door of her quarters, they gathered as much jewelry as they could from one of the rooms, then hurried out the front door of the palace.

Favonius saw Thomasina and Calla looking around as they hurried across the palace grounds. He picked them up, though they were even heavier than before.

"What do you think is going to happen when Psyche sees her husband?" Calla asked her sister.

"If I know our little sister, she will be so frightened, her husband will look like a monster even if he is not."

Calla laughed. "She probably won't even look at him. She'll try to stab him with her eyes closed."

They laughed.

"She doesn't have the nerve or the strength to kill anyone. If she tries, her husband, whoever he is, will awaken, see her with the knife in her hand, take it, and kill her."

"And then he will come looking for us to blame."

"Which is why we must not go back to our parents' palace. That is where Psyche's husband would look for us. Let us return to our husbands and offer to give them some of our jewels in exchange for divorces."

As Favonius put the sisters on the mountaintop, they did not know he had heard every word. He wanted to warn Psyche but knew she would not believe that her sisters, her blood kin, would be so deceitful and treacherous. Thomasina and Calla, however, deserved to be punished for their evil. Favonius would find the way to do that.

Cupid Exposed

Once Psyche was alone, her resolve vanished. How could she be contemplating killing her husband? He had been nothing but kind to her. She had riches; she lived in a palace of unsurpassed beauty. Her husband loved her with more passion than any other man could have.

Yet, he came to her only at night, leaving her alone and lonely during the daylight hours. Of what use were the beautiful gowns if no one saw her in them? Of what use were the brilliant jewels if no one saw them on her? Of what use were the beautiful palace gardens if she walked them, day after day, by herself? Of what use was her life if there was no one with whom she could share the day as well as the night?

Everything would be perfect if only she could see her husband's face. But he said he would go away if she ever did. How ugly and hideous could he be? Would all the love she had for him vanish when she saw his face? Psyche did not think she was that superficial.

She sat on the edge of her bed, the lamp and the knife on the floor at her feet. But what if he were everything her sisters had said he was? There was only one way to know for sure. She would look at him. He said he would leave her forever, but if he loved her as much as he said he did, how could he bear to leave her? She didn't think he would.

The time had come. For too long she had permitted him to dictate the terms of their relationship. Who did he think he was that he, and he alone, decided when she could see him?

Having made her decision, Psyche put the lamp under the bed and the knife beneath her pillow. She undressed, got into bed, and waited in the darkness.

Not much time passed before the double doors to the balcony opened. Psyche heard her husband's footsteps as he crossed the room. Her body tensed as he got into bed and took her in his arms. She felt his lips on her cheek and then her mouth, and they were as warm and sweet as they had been all the other nights.

Those are the lips of a human, she told herself, her body starting to relax. She took him in her arms and her fingers caressed his chest, waist, hips, and legs. Gently she touched his face, her fingers outlining his eyes, nose, and mouth.

This is no serpent in the guise of a man, she reassured herself, and flung her arms tightly around his neck, drawing him into the full beauty of her nakedness. On all other nights, he had made love to her. But on this one, excited to know that her husband was no monster and excited that she was, at long last, going to see his face, it was she who made love to him.

Cupid was startled by this new intensity of passion, startled but pleased. She had never given to him of herself so wholly. Her passion inflamed his. Then his inflamed hers, and their shared passion expanded until they felt like it enveloped the world. Finally, like stars bursting into myriad trails of light, they erupted in tears of gratitude for the other and for the passion.

They lay next to each other, exhausted but happy. Psyche wanted him to see the smile on her face and the wonder in her eyes. And she wanted to see those emotions on his face. The vocabularies of joy and awe were not written in words but in the eyes. One look into his eyes would tell her more about how much he loved her than all the words of love in the dictionaries of every language.

She closed her eyes and pretended to sleep. She waited until his breathing was regular. She reached out gently and touched his face with her fingertips. He did not move.

Slowly, quietly, she slipped from beneath the bedcovers and knelt down. She found the lamp and lit it. Then she took the knife in her other hand—just in case.

The lamp trembled in her hand as she stood up. She held it high enough so that its light shone on the face of her husband.

"Oh!" she exclaimed. She could not believe who she was gazing on. Could it be? Could it be that her husband was the god Cupid? It had to be. No mortal man could be so beautiful. His thick, curly hair was the color of sunlight. His face was strong, but a gentleness was on his lips. From his shoulders, wings arched upward like soft desire. The rest of his body was as smooth and beautiful as desire fulfilled.

Even the lamp knew on whom it was shining, and its flame began dancing back and forth with joy. The knife knew, also, and, turned its edge away from Cupid, then twisted out of Psyche's hand and fell to the floor, next to Cupid's bow and quiver of arrows.

Psyche saw her husband's sacred weapons. She stooped down to look at the arrows more closely. She pulled one out and touched the golden tip with a thumb. But she pressed too hard and pierced the skin.

Her love for her husband was already great, but now that she knew who he was, now that the potion from the arrow mixed with her blood, her love for him knew no bounds.

The lamp wanted to show its passion for the god, wanted to touch that beautiful body, and it spurted a drop of oil onto Cupid's shoulder.

The god awoke with a cry and sat up. He looked up to see Psyche gazing at him with ardent passion. Quickly he got out of bed, ran across the room to the balcony, and spread his wings.

"Please! Don't go!" Psyche shouted, running after him. As Cupid rose into the air, Psyche jumped and grabbed his right ankle. Cupid beat his wings furiously as he struggled to rise higher. He shook his leg, trying to dislodge Psyche. Finally, as he flew low over the meadow, her grasp weakened and she fell to the ground, crying.

Cupid alighted in a tree to catch his breath. He looked down on her. "Oh, Psyche. I disobeyed my mother, Venus, for you. She wanted me to have you fall in love with someone utterly unworthy of you. But I fell in love with you instead. I know now how foolish I was to have done so, to have disobeyed my mother. You would not believe your feelings of love for me. Instead, you listened to your evil sisters and let them convince you that I was a monster, when you knew in your heart that I was not. I warned you about them, but you would not listen. Now, I will do as I told you."

He flew away into the night.

Now, I'm going to have to put the story on pause because I know you have a question, and I know what the question is. Because Cupid had wings growing out of his shoulders, and Psyche had been hugging him every night, why hadn't she felt his wings? Why did she find out he had wings only after she looked at him in the light from the lamp?

I had that same question, and I asked the story about it. The story scratched its head and looked very confused. A story hates to be wrong, but it finally had to admit that it did not know why Psyche had never felt Cupid's wings. The only reason I could come up with was that Psyche's arms were short and they could only reach around Cupid's neck. The story liked that and gave me a high five. However, if that explanation doesn't work for you—well, you should come up with another one and put it in the story. Stories don't like to admit when they need help, but I know from experience that when you give it to them, they are very grateful. I have saved a whole lot of stories from oblivion.

Now, let's find out how Psyche is doing.

Psyche's Despair

Psyche lay in the grass where she had fallen, sobbing. She did not understand why Cupid had left her. Neither did she understand what she had done wrong. Yes, he had told her not to look at his face, but why was that so important? Did he expect her to love him and never know what he looked like, never to gaze into his eyes? Not only was that unfair, it was not realistic. Even the blind longed to see the faces of loved ones. How much more intense the longing of one who was sighted and yet forbidden to see?

But who was she to question a god? Especially the god of love. She had disobeyed a god's command, but she had not known he was a god when he commanded her not to look on him. If he had told her he was a god, of course she would have obeyed. But he had not. He had kept her in ignorance of his true identity. Did he not understand that what is forbidden to mortals is what they will crave the most?

But none of that mattered now. Cupid had left her. Now there was an emptiness inside her as great as her love for him. How was she supposed to continue living when her reason for living had left her?

She returned to the palace to look for her sisters. They had said they would help her kill her monstrous husband. Psyche looked in all the rooms but her sisters were not there. But in one of the rooms, she noticed that practically all the jewelry was missing.

How foolish she had been to believe them. Her husband had warned her about them, but she had refused to believe him. She had also ignored all she knew about Thomasina and Calla and how they had always been jealous of her, how they had never cared for anyone except themselves.

Betrayed by her sisters and abandoned by Cupid, Psyche could not bear to remain in the palace another moment. Not only was there no life for her at the palace, there was no life for her anywhere now.

Sun had begun his day and, eager as always to see Psyche, he had just risen above the mountains surrounding the valley when she walked across the meadow and into the woods. Her head was bowed, her shoulders slumped, and tears poured down her face.

Sun watched as she emerged from the woods and continued toward the river, whose currents were so dangerous even fish were afraid to swim in it. Realizing what Psyche was intent on doing, Sun shouted, "Psyche! Psyche!" But he was too far away. She could not hear him.

Unable to do anything to stop her, Sun did not want to watch. Vowing never again to let his emotions get involved in the affairs of humans, he closed his eyes.

When Psyche reached the river, she did not hesitate. She leaped into the furious, roiling waters. However, the river owed its existence to the god she despaired of ever seeing again. But the river knew him better under his other names, Eros and Phanes. From him light had first emanated; it was he who had set the universe in motion and created the sun, moon, sky, and earth. Such was the power of love that it banished primeval chaos. The waters, beasts, winds, trees, and birds remembered Eros and how he chose to enter the affairs of humans in the guise of Cupid, son of Venus, and they would never harm the one he had chosen as his beloved. Nor would they allow her to harm herself. So the river drew itself up into a wave, lifting Psyche and placing her gently back on the land.

Psyche lay on the ground, sobbing. If she could not kill herself, what she was supposed to do? Was it possible for someone to cry for her entire life? Were there that many tears in her body? She knew there were.

The sound of crying attracted the attention of Pan, the god of sheep and goats, pastures and woodlands. He liked to dance in nature while playing on pipes of reeds, which are called—what else?—panpipes, of course. Pan loved women, but with the legs and feet of a goat and with horns growing from his head, he was quite ugly. He was so ugly that people were frightened when they saw him and would go into a *pan*ic.

More than all the gods, Pan knew what it was like to love and have that love rejected. Seeing Psyche lying in the grasses, sobbing, he knew that crying of such violence came only from love unfulfilled.

He went to her, knelt beside her, and said quietly, "Beautiful lady. I am old and I have loved much. Alas, to no avail. No one will have me because the sincerity and strength of my love is not enough to overcome my ugliness. You would think a lifetime of loving and not being loved in return would have made me bitter. But it has not. I believe that one day I will find the one who will love me as I love her.

"I know your heart is aching in grief, but the cure is not to kill yourself. You must find the one you love. Go. Do not sit here crying. Go. Your beloved will not be stubborn and foolish forever."

Psyche continued sobbing. When her sobbing eventually slowed, she realized Pan was right. Why should she be miserable for the rest of her life? Better to search everywhere for Cupid than feel sorry for herself. Though he lived on Olympus, he came to the world of mortals often to create as well as destroy love. Who could say that she would not see him on one of his visits?

In the distance she heard the sound of panpipes. Smiling, she arose and began walking away from the river.

Psyche Visits Her Sisters

Psyche had not gone very far before she felt a gentle wind. She smiled as Favonius picked her up.

"Are you taking me to Cupid?" she asked hopefully.

"No," Favonius responded. "I have some unfinished business with your sisters, and I need your help."

"I will be more than happy to help you," Psyche said firmly.

Favonius told her everything he had heard Thomasina and Calla say. Then he told her what he wanted her to do, and she agreed.

West Wind carried her into the kingdom adjacent to the one over which her parents ruled. There he set her down outside the dark doors of a small mansion.

When the door opened in response to Psyche's knock, there stood her sister Thomasina.

"Psyche?" Thomasina asked in disbelief.

"Oh, Sister!" Psyche exclaimed and threw herself into her sister's arms.

"I thought—" Thomasina stopped herself.

Psyche looked at her through narrowed eyes. "Thought what? That I was dead?"

"No, no." She laughed nervously. "I . . . I . . . well, I did not think you, my baby sister, would have the courage to kill a monster."

"Ah, Sister. My husband is no monster."

"Then who is he?"

"He is the god Cupid."

"Cupid!" Thomasina exclaimed. "Of course. Who else could live in a palace filled with such riches? Oh, Psyche! You silly girl! You should have figured that out immediately."

"Alas, dear sister. Not only did I not, but the god awoke and saw me standing over him with a knife. He glared at me and said, 'I divorce you. I will marry your oldest sister instead. She will know how to appreciate me.' And with those words, he flew away and out of my life. Oh, Sister! My heart is broken."

Thomasina could not believe what she was hearing.

Cupid wanted her to be his wife? She would be the owner of all those jewels, that palace, and invisible servants to do whatever she wanted.

She ran to her husband. "My lord, I have sad news. My sister has arrived to tell me that our parents are dead. I must go home at once."

Her husband agreed, of course.

Thomasina hurried away and ran past Psyche, who was still standing in the doorway. "Thank you, Sister, for being so dumb," Thomasina said, as she stepped outside.

Immediately Favonius swept Thomasina up and carried her to the mountaintop. But this time, he left her there.

A sharp and cold wind arose. It was Aquilo, North Wind, who had come at the bidding of Favonius. Aquilo blew with all the malice he had learned from the lord of the underworld, and before Thomasina knew what was happening to her, Aquilo swept her off the mountaintop and she fell down the steep mountainside. The sharp rocks and crags cut and slashed her body. She was dead before she reached the bottom.

Then Favonius carried Psyche to the mansion where her sister Calla lived. Psyche told the same story to her. Calla had the same thoughts and said the same words Thomasina had. Favonius carried Calla to the mountaintop and she met the same fate as her sister.

Favonius thanked Psyche for her help; she thanked him for his. Then she continued on her way.

Cupid Goes Home

When we last saw Cupid he had just given Psyche a little self-righteous lecture and was on his way to Olympus. But he kept looking back at Psyche, lying in the grasses where she had fallen. It was all he could do not to turn around, go to her, and apologize for being such a fathead. He was surprised that he still wanted to be with her. He had thought his leaving would punish her for not obeying him. Only now did he realize: by leaving home was also punishing himself.

As much as he wanted to return to her, he couldn't. Well, he could have, but he was acting like a stubborn boy, unable to admit that he had made a mistake. He thought it would show weakness if he went back to her. Even worse, he was afraid that if she found out that seeing her in pain could make him change his mind, she would be in control of the relationship. He could not allow that.

Why had she ruined things? It had been a perfect relationship. He had given her more riches than any mortal had ever seen; he had given her servants to wait on her. Every night he had made love to her. Why hadn't all that been enough?

Now he had to face Venus. How could he explain going against her wishes? He couldn't. There was no justification for disobeying his mother.

When Cupid reached Olympus, he landed in a large

field near the palace he shared with Venus. He looked for signs of activity but saw nothing. Perhaps she was away. He hoped so. All he wanted to do was go to his chambers, get in bed, and go to sleep. He was not feeling well.

But he was a god, and gods did not get ill, though what else could he call the pain he felt in his abdomen, the aching in his head, not to mention the general malaise that had come over him? His spirit felt heavy, as if he were lying beneath the ground, unable to move and, strangely, without any desire to. What he really wanted to do was curl up in bed and cry.

He made his way slowly to the palace. He peered in windows until he found his mother, in her chambers, receiving a massage from Oizys. The goddess of pain smiled as she watched Cupid hurry to the other side of the palace, where his chambers were.

When he reached his rooms, he took off his bow and quiver of arrows. Then he lay on his bed, and despite his resolve not to, he began to cry.

Oizys's Revenge

The goddess of pain and misery was one of the most attractive of the deities. She had long reddish-brown hair, eyes as green as new grass in early spring, and thin, delicate lips. She always dressed in beautiful gowns and chandelier earrings that matched whatever she had on. Given that she was as beautiful as any of the other goddesses, with the exception of Venus, she resented that there were no stories about her as there were about practically all the other deities.

But she knew why. How could there be stories about someone whom the other deities avoided? Mortals knew that Oizys walked among them, because all of them had been deceived by her appearance and ended up in situations that promised happiness but delivered pain and misery.

Venus was the only deity who would have anything to do with Oizys. That was because Venus did not mind the pain of Oizys's massages, even when it seemed like Oizys was going to break a few bones.

While Oizys was grateful that Venus appreciated her services, she also resented the goddess of love. How could she not? Mortals adored Venus, wrote poems and sang songs about her. They thought love was the greatest of experiences. But where would they be without pain and misery? It was pain that forced them to look at their lives, learn from their experiences, and grow. Even in their love relationships, they had to be made miserable by the absence of a beloved before they learned the value of that beloved. But did people dedicate temples to her? Were there priests and priestesses performing rituals in her honor? Were dances choreographed to her glory? No, no, and no!

This was why she never passed up an opportunity to make Venus miserable, like when she had told the goddess about Psyche. But she had something even better in mind today. All she had to do was manipulate Venus into asking her about it.

Oizys poured warmed and scented oil on Venus's back and began to rub it in with sure, strong strokes. With each stroke she sighed deeply.

"Are you all right, Oizys?" Venus asked quietly.

"Who, me? I'm fine."

"Then why are you sighing like something is wrong?"

"I apologize, Goddess. I did not know I was sighing."

Venus turned over and looked at Oizys, concern in her eyes. "What's wrong? You know you can tell me."

Oizys shook her head. "I am grateful for your concern, Goddess, but it is nothing. Please. Turn so I can give you a good, deep massage."

Venus shook her head. "Not until you tell me what's bothering you."

Oizys sighed again, this time more deeply than ever. "I hesitate to do so. I am afraid you will be angry with me when I am nothing more than the messenger."

"This is something that concerns me?" Venus said, sitting up. "Speak, Oizys. You have my word. I will not be angry with you for being the bearer of news I should hear, whether I like it or not."

Oizys was smiling to herself. How easily the goddess had taken the bait. "If you insist."

"I insist."

"Very well." Still, Oizys said nothing.

Venus was getting impatient. "What were you going to say?"

"Excuse me, Goddess. I was thinking of how to put it."

"Just say it. I'm not someone who needs to be coddled."

"Well, what I report may or may not be true. It is what I have been hearing as I go about every day. There seems to be a scandal in the Venus household. I am here almost every day and I have seen no scandal, but this is what is being said."

"Be specific. What scandal are you talking about?"

"Have you seen your son recently?"

Venus did not want to answer. She had not seen him in quite some time. "Well, no," she answered reluctantly.

"Ah. Then perhaps it is true."

"What's true?"

"The rumor is that Cupid is having an affair with some young woman. He is with her every night, and during the daylight hours, he is thinking about her. As a result, mortals are not falling in love with each other, or breaking up, for that matter. Those who speak of such things are saying that you have neglected your temples and they have fallen into disrepair. Because neither you nor Cupid are carrying out your duties, husbands and wives no longer care for each other; people ignore their friends and their children. Pleasure, Grace, and Wit are disappearing from societies. Mortals are becoming less and less capable of knowing, or even caring, about beauty. If beauty is dethroned from its place in the hearts of mortals, they will find it repulsive to express even the slightest affection for each other, and chaos will engulf them."

Venus had heard little after the first sentence. "My son has a lover, has he? Who is it? One of the nymphs? Or, maybe one of the hours—Auros, perhaps. No, not her. She has more lovers than she has time for. Perhaps one of the muses. No. Apollo would not permit one of them to take up with my son. It couldn't be one of the graces, could it? No, they are my attendants. Neither he nor they would dare! Do you know who it is?"

"I am not sure, Goddess. I know what I heard but I found it hard to believe."

"What did you hear?"

"Well, they are saying that your son has fallen madly in love with a mortal named Psyche. Isn't she the one you told your son to make miserable?" Oizys asked innocently.

"What?" Venus roared, getting off the table. "My son and Psyche! How dare she take my son from me!"

"Oh, Goddess," Oizys said sweetly. "Don't upset yourself. It is my understanding that your son will return to you with your first grandchild."

"What!" Venus exploded. "She's pregnant? I don't believe it! I refuse to believe it, and I won't believe it until I hear it from Cupid's lips and his lips alone." She stopped. "Is that why I have not seen my son of late? Has he been avoiding me? If he has been seeing that Psyche behind my back, it's not surprising that he doesn't want to see me. Where could he be?"

"I believe he might be in his chambers," Oizys offered sweetly.

Venus dressed hurriedly and went to the other side of the palace and into Cupid's chambers. He was lying in bed, the blanket pulled up to his chin, staring at the ceiling.

"You!" Venus roared. "How dare you disobey me! How dare you take up with the very woman mortals think is more beautiful than I am. How dare you fall in love with my enemy. I don't understand what got into you. Don't you know that I can ask Jupiter to take that bow and those arrows from you, have another son, and make *him* the god of love?

"I should have known better than to trust you. All you've ever thought about is doing what you want to do. Say something! Explain yourself!"

But Cupid just lay there, depressed, staring up at the ceiling.

"Say something!" Venus yelled.

Cupid said nothing.

"Very well," Venus said under her breath. "Keep quiet, because there is nothing you can say that would justify what you've done to me. But it's my fault, all my fault. I indulged you all your life. You've been a brat since the day you were born. You've enjoyed destroying relationships and getting people to fall in love with the most unsuitable persons on the planet. You made a fool of Apollo, not to mention your poor mother. Well, now it's your time to rue what you've done. You allowed yourself to fall in love with the woman who dared usurp my position in the hearts of mortals. When I get done with her, you'll be sorry you dared disobey me."

Venus hurried away from Cupid's chambers and out the door of the palace. As she rushed toward the center of Olympus, where she knew she would find the other deities, she noticed people snickering as she went by. It seemed that all of Olympus had known about Cupid and Psyche, everyone except her! How dare they make fools of her!

When she reached the center of Olympus, she saw her mother-in-law, Juno, the wife of Jupiter and goddess of women, and her aunt Ceres, the earth goddess.

"Venus," said Juno, "you look so angry. A scowl like that can ruin your beauty."

"Juno. Ceres. You are just the two I came seeking. If you tell me what I need to know, my beauty will be preserved."

"Please tell us what is troubling you," Ceres replied.

"Would you happen to know where I might find a mortal creature named Psyche?"

Juno and Ceres put their hands before their mouths to hide their smiles, but Venus noticed.

"I see you have heard of her and the scandal she has brought to my family by her affair with Cupid."

Juno patted Venus lightly on the shoulder. "My dear. You must not take such matters so seriously. What harm has been done? Surely, you, of all people, cannot consider it a crime for Cupid to make love with a beautiful young woman."

"Oh, I know how hard it is to see one's child grow up," Ceres added. "In case you hadn't noticed, Cupid is no longer a boy. He's a young man, and it is only right that he should be curious about young women, and what young man, even if he is a god, could resist someone as stunningly beautiful as Psyche?"

"Ceres is right, you know," Juno put in. "She and I were talking about the situation last night. We found it strange that a woman of your vast experience and knowledge would be sticking your nose into Cupid's life in this way. What he does is his business now."

"And, surely, you can't believe that what has happened has been all Psyche's doing," Ceres added. "Cupid had as much, if not more, to do with this than she did."

"To be honest, Venus, you should be ashamed of yourself. You take such pleasure in arousing others to love. Do you really want us to believe that you want to deny your own son the same pleasure?"

Juno and Ceres were not being totally honest. They were afraid to say anything negative about Cupid lest he shoot arrows into them. They were not going to risk his ire by telling Venus where Psyche was.

Venus was more angry now than before, and she walked away without a word.

Psyche Looks for Help

Psyche had been going from town to town looking for Cupid without success. On this particular day, she was walking through the countryside when she saw a temple high atop a steep hill. Thinking Cupid might be there, she made the arduous climb and went inside.

She was surprised to see sheaves of wheat, ears of barley and corn, scattered across the temple floor. Perhaps the strong winds of a storm had blown the offerings from the altar.

Psyche thought this must be a temple devoted to the worship of Ceres, the goddess responsible for the fruits of the earth. Hoping the goddess would take pity on her and tell her where to find Cupid, Psyche began cleaning up, sorting the offerings into groups and arranging them neatly.

It just so happened that Ceres had come to Earth that day to visit the very temple Psyche was tidying.

"Poor child," Ceres said softly, as she came inside and saw Psyche. "Venus is very angry with you. In all eternity, I have never seen her so furious. She wants to take revenge on you for loving her son. I am moved deeply that you have taken the time to neaten my temple when you should be hiding in fear of your life."

Psyche prostrated herself at the goddess's feet and began weeping. "Oh, Goddess! By all that is sacred to you—the corn and grains of the fields, the rites of planting and harvest—in the name of your daughter Proserpine, who was taken by the god of the dead to his terrible realm, along with the green of the land and warmth of the sun, but who returns for six months each year, bringing with her light and joy and the fruition of the earth, I implore you to allow me to hide here until the wrath of the goddess Venus subsides."

"Ah, child. Your plight brings sorrow to my heart. I wish I could help you, but Venus is my niece and, despite herself, one of my dearest friends. I cannot offer you shelter here. In fact, I must ask you to leave at once. I shudder to think what will happen if Venus ever learns that you were in my presence and I did not bring you to her. You must go this instant."

Psyche left, sadder now than when she had come.

As she came down from the mountain, she saw, in the valley below, another temple hidden in a grove of trees. Offerings of beautiful scarves and gowns hung from tree branches and the temple doorposts. Psyche recognized that she was at a temple devoted to Juno. Surely, if any goddess would come to her aid, it would be the goddess of women and childbirth. Was not Psyche a woman? Was she not pregnant with a child by a god?

Psyche went inside and began to pray: "Goddess of childbirth, who is also known as Juno the Protectress. Please guard me and keep me from danger. I am very, very tired. I have wandered for days, lost and afraid. But you, Goddess, you help women who are pregnant, and I am with child. Please protect me and the child I carry within me."

Juno appeared in response to Psyche's prayer. "Oh, dear child! It would give me the deepest pleasure to protect you. Alas, divine etiquette does not permit me. I cannot go against the wishes of Venus. She's married to my son and I've loved her as if she were my own child. Now, I must ask you to leave at once. I shudder to think how deeply hurt Venus would be if she knew you stood in my presence and I did not have you brought to her."

Psyche left Juno's temple more despondent than ever. If two such powerful goddesses turned their backs on her, what was she to do? With tears pouring down her face, she knew the answer. She had to submit to Venus and hope the goddess would be merciful.

Venus Looks for Psyche

Having been betrayed by her own son and laughed at by Ceres and Juno, there remained only one individual Venus could trust to help her find Psyche, but she needed Jupiter's permission.

Jupiter was the god of gods, the highest of the high, the boss, the CEO, Big Daddy, and anything else along those lines you might want to add. He lived in a palace at the center of a complex of buildings. Here was where all the business of Olympus and Earth was recorded. This was also the place where the deities came together for monthly meetings to discuss what was happening on Earth and what they should do about those events of which they disapproved.

Because he was who he was, Jupiter knew all that had taken place between Cupid and Psyche. And, if the truth be known, he was a little upset with himself that he had somehow overlooked a young woman that beautiful. And if Cupid didn't stop acting like a mama's boy fairly soon, Jupiter would not hesitate to let Psyche know how much pleasure her beauty gave him.

He looked out the window and saw Venus making her way across the plaza. She was probably on her way to ask him to do something about Psyche. He was disappointed that Venus was so angry. He wanted to tell her it was time to let her son grow up, but Venus was too angry to listen to reason. The only person who could make Venus change her behavior was the very one sitting in his chambers feeling sorry for himself. If Cupid could not stand up to his mother, Jupiter would accomplish nothing by doing it for him.

Just then the guards at the doors to the throne room announced, "Lord Jupiter! The goddess Venus requests an audience with you."

"Admit her at once!"

Venus walked rapidly across the long marble floor to Jupiter, who sat on his golden throne.

"Father!"

"My daughter! It is good to see you, as always. What brings you here today?"

"I come seeking your permission."

Jupiter raised his thick brows. "If you are asking my permission for something, it must be a matter of great and grave importance."

"Nothing has ever been more important to me."

"Please continue."

"I am asking for the services of Mercury, the town crier of Olympus, to help me in a matter of urgency."

Jupiter wanted to ask what it was she wanted Mercury to do, but he decided that the less he knew, the better. "So it shall be. Your request is granted."

"Thank you, Father." Venus hurried from the room.

Of all the gods, Mercury was the only one who did not have a palace. The reason was simple: he was always so busy flying from one end of Olympus to the other, delivering messages, he would not have had time to spend in a palace had he had one. Instead, he generally spent the night at whichever palace he delivered the last message of the day. Everyone was always happy to have Mercury as an overnight guest, because he knew the best gossip on Olympus and on Earth. Down there, on Earth, the Four Winds went everywhere and saw and heard everything and were always happy to share anything they knew. The deities loved Mercury because he was not shy about telling everything he knew about anyone.

As Venus walked down the steps from Jupiter's palace, she wondered where she was going to find Mercury. He could be anywhere on Olympus or down on Earth. And even if he was on Olympus, he flew so fast it was hard to see him sometimes.

Venus had just reached street level when who should appear at her side but Mercury.

"You're just the one I was coming to look for," Venus said, smiling.

Those walking by at that moment and seeing the smile Venus gave Mercury had all the proof they thought they needed to confirm the rumor that Mercury was Cupid's father. But there were many others who were convinced the father was Mars. This is a matter I would pursue further if the story wasn't telling me it's not important who Cupid's father was. I'm not convinced that's true, but if I stop and argue the matter, the story will go on without me, and I can't have that.

"Oh, I know," Mercury answered. "I've been waiting for you to ask for my services."

"Oh?"

"The first time I saw that little hussy Psyche, I knew she was going to be trouble. Never in all eternity would I have thought Cupid would permit her to rule his heart. And I am outraged that she allowed mortals to believe she had come to replace you! How dare she!"

Venus smiled. At least one of the gods understood. "I'm glad you feel the way you do. What I want you to do is simple: go down to Earth and announce that I will give a reward to the person who finds Psyche."

"And what shall I say the reward is?"

"A kiss from my lips."

Mercury raised his eyebrows. "I can't imagine you bestowing a kiss on some dirty peasant."

"Juno forbid! I will tell any lie I need to in order to get my hands on Psyche."

"Would you consider a kiss or two, or more, for your coconspirator in this enterprise?" he asked flirtatiously.

"Well, after this affair between Psyche and my son is settled, I will be more than happy to show you how grateful I am. And as you know, I have a weakness for a god with wings."

Mercury blushed. "Then, the longer I linger here, the longer it is until this sordid affair between your son and Psyche ends." With those words, he flew down to Earth.

Mercury's feet were hardly on the ground before he shouted, "Yo! Listen up! Everybody! Listen up."

People gathered around him quickly.

"The goddess Venus is offering a reward to the person who captures Psyche and takes her to the goddess's temple."

"What's the reward?" someone in the crowd wanted to know.

Mercury's face lit up. "Ah, yes. The reward. The reward is a kiss from the mouth of Venus herself."

The thought of receiving kisses from Venus excited some in the crowd, but not most. They were being asked to betray Psyche. That was a lot to ask of them. But they were not sure she was still alive. The last time they had seen her, she was on her way to the top of the mountain, where, they were convinced, she met her death at the hands of her monster husband. But Triple A (remember him, the inventor of sunglasses?) said he thought he had seen her wandering through the countryside, except that the sad and distraught figure he had seen looked more like a ghost than a person.

Just then a woman called out, "That's who that was! Earlier today I saw someone I thought was her but I said to myself, 'Can't be Psyche. She's dead.' But now that you mention it, I believe it was her!"

"Where did you see her?" Mercury wanted to know.

"She was coming out of the grove where Juno's temple stands."

The crowd did not have to go far along the road to Juno's temple before they came upon Psyche sitting beneath a tree.

The young woman they saw bore only a faint resemblance to the Psyche they had known. Where Psyche's hair had been silken straight and shone with blackness, this young woman's hair was dull and lay in tangles like brambles down her back. Where Psyche's face had glowed, this young woman's face was dirty. Where Psyche's eyes had gleamed with life, this young woman's eyes looked as if she had tasted the most bitter dregs of sorrow.

"Why do you stare so with your mouths agape? Do you not recognize me?" Psyche asked, standing up. "I am the one who, not too long ago, you thought was more beautiful than Venus. Look on me and see what happens when one incurs the wrath of a deity."

The crowd was silent. They were ashamed that they had once lain awake at nights gazing at the image of Psyche they carried in their minds.

However, a few in the crowd saw that Psyche's beauty had not been taken from her. It had merely been transformed. To them she seemed more beautiful than ever because the challenges of living were writing themselves on her face.

Triple A stepped out of the crowd and bowed before Psyche. "My lady, please forgive me," he began. "We have no desire to turn you over to Venus, not even for a kiss from her lips. But what the gods command, we mortals must do."

"I am weary of this ordeal. I am ready to meet my fate," Psyche responded firmly.

Venus and Psyche

On Olympus Venus waited impatiently for Mercury to bring her news of Psyche's capture. Venus's chariot stood outside her palace, so she could go to Earth immediately upon hearing that Psyche was now hers. To insure that her son would not interfere, she had locked the door to his chambers. If he still wanted Psyche after she was done, he could have her. But she doubted Cupid would want a dead woman.

Just then, Mercury ran into her palace. "The deed has been accomplished. Psyche is on her way to your temple."

"Thank you, Mercury. You have been a true friend."

"I am delighted that I could be of service. Now please excuse me. I have a lot of gossip to catch up on."

"And to tell about me, I'm sure."

"But of course." Mercury smiled as he hurried out the door.

Never had Venus flown so rapidly through the air, but she wanted to be sitting in her throne chair at her temple when Psyche arrived.

Since the day Psyche had gone to the mountaintop, the people had returned to their worship of Venus. Her temple had been cleaned and scrubbed many times until it gleamed so brightly in the midday sun, no one could gaze on it directly. When people approached the temple, they did so with heads bowed, which Venus thought was appropriate.

Psyche arrived, head bowed as she approached Venus. When she was a respectful distance from the goddess, Psyche prostrated herself.

"Goddess," she began, but Venus stopped her.

"I don't want to hear a word you have to say. Stand up so I can look at you."

Psyche rose.

"Look at me!" Venus commanded.

Psyche raised her bowed head. Too afraid to look directly at the goddess, her gaze fixed on a point over Venus's left shoulder.

"Whatever did my son see in you? You are so ordinary looking. There are serving girls in your father's palace more beautiful than you. What did you do to Cupid that he would look at you and find you beautiful? Is there some wicked seer in this land who made a potion for you to give to my son?"

"My lady, I—"

"Shut up! Did I tell you that you could speak?"

Psyche shook her head.

"Good! Now, tell me this. There is an ugly rumor that you are carrying Cupid's child. Tell me this is not so."

"To say that would be a lie," Psyche said softly.

"Oh, my Juno!" Venus exclaimed. "You are pregnant? Yes or no? Are you pregnant with Cupid's child?"

"Yes," Psyche responded, this time looking directly at Venus.

"Oh no!" Venus screamed. "How could this have happened? Well, I know how it happened, but I don't believe my son would do this to me. Me, a grandmother? I'm much too young to have a grandchild. Much too young! And you will not turn me into a grandmother. You may call yourself the wife of Cupid, but no marriage ceremony took place in my temple, did it?"

Psyche shook her head.

"Then, I am not a grandmother and your child will be a bastard."

With those words, Psyche began crying softly.

"Oh, don't start crying just yet! Save your tears for what I am going to do to you!"

Venus called for the attendants of the temple and whispered something to them. They hurried away. Shortly they returned carrying heavy bags on their shoulders.

"The only way someone as sorry looking as you will ever get a husband is through hard work. This is a test to see just how diligent you are."

Venus motioned to the attendants. They opened the bags, and onto the floor, they dumped pile after pile of grains and seeds—wheat, barley, millet, lentils, beans, poppy, and vetch.

"Now," Venus ordered, "mix them all together!"

The attendants did so. When they finished, the pile had grown until it almost touched the domed ceiling.

"Your task, you piece of vermin, is to sort out the different kinds of grains and seeds and to put each in its own pile. Oh, yes. Have it done by the time the sun goes down. Now I have a wedding to attend." Venus went outside, got in her carriage, and flew off.

Psyche slumped to the floor. Why hadn't she been content with her life? Allowing people to stare at her had not been so awful, had it? What were a few moments of being looked at compared to the wrath of a goddess? She could not do what Venus asked even if she lived a hundred years. And so, Psyche lay there sobbing.

It just so happened that an ant was making its way across the floor at that very moment. Something appeared in its path. To the ant, whatever it was would not be an obstacle. If he could not find a way around it, then he would go over. If it was too high to go over, he would find a way under.

However, when the ant got close to the object, he stopped. He stared. He had not seen anything so beautiful since the day he had seen a tiny portion of Psyche's big toe. He looked closer. Could it be? Could it? Oh, my Jupiter! It was! Psyche's big toe! This was Psyche's foot!

But before the ant could jump up and down and start shouting with joy, he heard sobbing. Quickly, he hurried up to Psyche's head.

"Oh, dear lady. What is making you weep?"

"The goddess Venus has commanded me to separate all the grains and seeds into separate piles according to their kind, and to be done by sunset. That is impossible!"

"How cruel the goddess is to you," the ant replied. "She is jealous of your beauty. Wipe your eyes and do not worry. What is impossible to a mortal is merely routine for ants."

Quickly, he called for all the ants in the area, and that was thousands. "Do you remember when I told you I had encountered the most beautiful creature in the world?"

All the ants agreed that they did.

"She needs our help. There is no telling what the goddess

Venus might do to her if she does not have this great mound of seeds and grains separated into their own piles by the time Sun goes to bed. Quickly, let us get to work!"

The ants swarmed over the huge mound. Grain by grain, seed by seed, they began carrying and sorting.

Although Sun had promised himself to stay out of the affairs of mortals, he could not let Psyche fail. He asked Night if she minded coming a little later. Night did not mind at all. Anything that was going to let her get a little more sleep was fine. So Sun delayed his going down until the ants had finished sorting the grains and seeds and putting them in piles of their own kind. Sun inspected each pile to make sure none of the ants had made a mistake and put a seed in a pile where it did not belong. But they were ants and would not have made a ridiculous mistake like that. Satisfied that all was as it should be, Sun resumed his journey downward.

It was evening when Venus returned. She was a little tipsy from having drunk too much champagne at the wedding. However, she was not too drunk to see that all the seeds and grains had been sorted into their proper piles.

"Who did you put a spell on to do this for you? Don't tell me! It doesn't matter. Tomorrow I will give you a task no one can do for you. For now, come with me! You will spend the night in my palace so I will know where you are!"

Psyche slept that night under the same roof as Cupid. She did not know this. Cupid, still lying on his bed, heard his mother return. Someone was with her, someone to whom his mother spoke with more anger than he had ever heard from her. There was only one person with whom his mother could be that angry. For the first time since he had returned to his mother's house, Cupid sat up, his mind and body alert.

Could it be? Was Psyche there?

Psyche's Second Task

Psyche slept well that night, even if her bed was the cold dirt floor of a narrow room in the basement. She had not expected to sleep at all, but she had. Although she feared what Venus would ask her to do next, she was also relieved to no longer be wandering aimlessly looking for Cupid. Maybe he was here in his mother's house and would come to her rescue. But what need would a god as beautiful as Cupid have of her? However, she had felt his love and was carrying his child. That had to mean something to him.

The sound of footsteps interrupted her reverie. The door opened. A servant holding a candle beckoned for Psyche to follow her. When they reached the main floor, Psyche blinked her eyes against the brightness of the light streaming through the palace windows. The servant put Psyche in a small room where there was a large bowl of fruit.

"You are to eat," the servant said, and then left.

Psyche had just finished the last piece of fruit when the door opened and Venus walked in.

"I'm glad to see that you ate. I wouldn't want you to faint and deprive me of my vengeance. Come! I don't know who helped you sort the grains and seeds, but whoever it was won't be able to help you today. Follow me."

Venus took Psyche into the countryside. They walked until they came to a grove of trees on the banks of a stream.

"You see those trees?" Venus said, pointing.

Psyche nodded.

"If you look closely, you will see sheep with fleece of gold."

Psyche nodded again.

"Bring me some of the wool," Venus commanded, and then left.

That seemed easy enough, and that was the problem. Venus would not have given her an easy task. Psyche walked closer to the grove to get a better look at the sheep. Their fleece was like finely spun gold, but on their heads were massive horns. They also had long, curved teeth from which dripped a thick, clear liquid. It looked like the poison Psyche had seen her father's physician take from a deadly reptile once.

Psyche understood now how Venus was going to have her killed. When she went to take the fleece, the sheep would stab her with their sharp horns while others would bite her and flood her body with the poison from their long teeth. If, by some chance, Psyche did the impossible and got fleece from the sheep, what would it matter? Tomorrow Venus would give her an even harder task. And if she succeeded at that one, there would be a task of greater difficulty the following day, and this would go on until one of the tasks resulted in her death.

"Why delay the inevitable?" she thought. If she killed herself, at least she could deny Venus the pleasure of bringing about her death.

Psyche looked at the river and thought about flinging herself in, then remembered the water's refusal to receive her before. But that was on Earth. This was Olympus. Perhaps this river would take pity on her.

As Psyche started toward the stream, Pan was at the far end of the meadow, cleaning his pipes. He saw Psyche, her head down and shoulders slumped, and he knew what she was going to do. He wanted to call out to her, but she was too far away. So he reached down and pulled from the ground a green reed like the ones of his pipes. He threw the reed as hard and far as he could. The reed landed in front of Psyche just as she reached the edge of the stream.

"Wait!" the reed said. "Please wait!"

Psyche stopped.

"This stream is sacred to the god Pan. He often sits beside it and listens to the melodies of the rushing water and then plays them on his pipes. If you drown yourself here, the only melodies the water will ever sing will be dirges and laments, and those will be the only melodies Pan will be able to play."

Psyche remembered how kind Pan had been to her and she remembered what he had said to her, and her self-pity vanished. She stepped back from the stream's edge.

"Thank you," the reed said. "Now listen carefully. The golden-fleeced sheep are very dangerous. They are most dangerous now, when the sun is shining on them. The heat makes them angry, and anyone who enters the grove will be gored to death by their horns, crushed by butts from their heads, or poisoned by their fangs. Wait until Sun begins his journey down from the top of the sky. The sheep, exhaused by the heat and their anger, will fall asleep. Then you can enter the grove and pick all the fleece you need from the briars the sheep have brushed against."

Psyche did as the reed told her. That evening she presented Venus with a lap full of golden fleece.

The goddess sneered. "You obviously had the help of someone for this task, also. Well, your ability to get others to take risks for you exceeds what I imagined. Let's see how you fare with what I have in store for you tomorrow."

One of Venus's servants took Psyche back to the basement and locked her in for the night. Psyche sat on the dirt floor, her back against the stone wall. She thought about how Pan had come to her rescue again. Favonius had enlisted her help in dealing with her sisters. Could it be that the gods and nature itself did not want Venus to succeed? That was almost too much to hope for, but could it be? The thought filled with her with such joy that she laughed aloud.

In the room above, Cupid lay on his bed. For a moment he thought he heard laughter, but who would feel such happiness in the house of his mother?

The Third Task

The next morning, the servant came and again took Psyche up to the small room, and like the morning before, there was a bowl of fruit, which she devoured. The servant then took her to the back of the palace, where Venus waited, a crystal goblet in one hand.

"I hope you slept well," Venus greeted Psyche. "You are going to need every ounce of strength and all your wits for what I have planned today."

"I slept very well, Goddess."

Venus did not like that answer, but she said, "Good! I am glad! Now, see that mountain?" She pointed at a nearby peak. "On it there is a river of rushing white water, the river Styx. Take this crystal goblet and fill it with cold water from the river." She stopped and laughed. "However, the water must be taken from the middle of the river, at the place where the river comes out of the underground."

Psyche nodded and took the goblet from Venus. The goddess sneered, then turned and walked away, laughter extending behind her like the train of a gown.

Psyche stood for a moment, despair threatening to make her its own yet again. However, before it could do so this time, Psyche remembered: only when she felt that she would have to accomplish a task alone did despair and self-pity overtake her. But she was not alone. And so she turned and started walking toward the mountain.

However, when Psyche reached the top of the mountain, she stared in disbelief. The river Styx began deep in the underworld and burst forth in a roaring torrent from a gaping hole in the mountain, which was guarded on both sides by dragons who never slept or blinked their eyes. And as the river tumbled and swirled and roiled down the rocky mountainside, it sang out: "Death! Death! Death! Be off! Be off!"

Unknown to Psyche and Venus, Jupiter had been watching. He was disappointed that Venus had allowed her anger to obliterate her common sense. It was as if she had married her soul to that of her son, and no mother should love her son in that way. While it was Cupid's task to free himself from his mother and marry his soul to Psyche's, someone had to keep Psyche alive until Cupid came to his senses.

"Aquila!" Jupiter called out.

The giant eagle, Jupiter's royal bird, heard his master's voice and flew down from his aerie, high on the highest mountains. Jupiter pointed to where Psyche stood on the bank of the river Styx, a crystal goblet in her hand. Aquila understood, for he, too, had been watching the drama between Venus and Psyche. If he was going to favor one over the other, it would be Psyche, because Cupid had helped him when Jupiter wanted Ganymede brought to Olympus to be his cupbearer.

The great bird flew swiftly and snatched the crystal goblet from Psyche's hand. However, being Jupiter's bird did not mean accomplishing the task was going to be easy. The dragons saw the eagle coming toward them, and he saw them. Aquila flew high. The dragons, baring their fangs, stretched their long necks into the sky and struck at the eagle with their three-forked tongues. The royal eagle folded his wings tightly against his body and, like an arrow from the bow of Apollo, shot down to the place in the mountain where the river poured forth.

But just as he reached it, the river stopped and said, "Who comes to steal my water? Leave now before I rise up and drown you."

"The goddess Venus has sent me," the eagle said. "She is concocting a love potion that requires only the purest of water, and what water is purer than that of the river Styx?"

The river, flattered that Venus needed it, filled the goblet. By this time, the dragons had located Aquila, and just as they struck at him again, the great bird raised himself into the air and flew back to where Psyche stood on the shore, watching in awe.

Aquila gave the goblet to Psyche.

"Thank you!" she said.

"You're welcome," the eagle responded. "I am Aquila, Jupiter's bird."

"Jupiter!" Psyche exclaimed.

"Jupiter," Aquila repeated. "Do you understand?"

Psyche nodded, and the magnificent bird flew back to his aerie.

This time, when Psyche returned to the palace and handed Venus the goblet filled with water from the mouth of the river Styx, she looked the goddess in the eye and smiled.

"I keep underestimating your powers, Witch!" Venus screamed, beside herself with rage. "Such powers as you have should belong only to a deity. No mortal should have access to the powers you have stolen from somewhere. You are a danger to mortals and deities. Tomorrow you die!"

Psyche was returned to the cold, dark room in the basement. As she lay down to sleep on the cold dirt floor, she thought she heard weeping from the room above hers.

Cupid's Tears

The story and I have been having a big argument. We are getting close to the end, and the story wants to hurry up and get there. I keep telling it that we will get to the end when we get there and not a minute sooner. Sometimes stories don't know the best way to tell themselves. That's especially true of some of the very old stories like this one. It has gotten used to being told one way, and I'm having a hard time getting the story to understand that people listen to stories differently than they did back in the year one hundred. People today are surrounded by stories. There are radio and television stations that do nothing but broadcast news, and what is news except stories? Then there are the stories people see in the movies and on television—love stories, funny stories, stories about murders, robberies, kidnappings, and on and on. People today probably know more about stories than people did in the year one hundred, which is why I know the people listening to this story have been wondering, "What's up with Cupid? The dude just dropped out of the story."

Well, no, he hasn't. The story says it has no idea what Cupid is doing, because I changed things. You remember the scene when Psyche took the lamp and looked at Cupid, and the oil dropped on him. Well, back in the year one hundred, the burn injured him so severely that he had to stay in bed until it healed. That might have made sense to folks back in one hundred, but people today would not believe something as lame as that. They would say Cupid was a wimp if he was going to go missing in action from a little burn. Plus, Psyche was much too fine to be wasting her time on someone who lets his mama push him around like he was still in a baby carriage. So I told the story this is not the year one hundred, and it can't be telling itself now the way it told itself then. And anyway, I'm doing the telling this time, so the story best sit down and listen.

When we last saw Cupid he was lying in bed, looking up at the ceiling, trying to figure out how things got so messed up. In the first place, he had thought that Psyche would be happy with him coming to see her every night. This proves that Cupid did not know anything about women. As much as most women love jewelry, fine clothes, and chocolate, they want to go places so they can show off their jewelry and clothes. They also want to go places so they can show off their husbands, or whomever they are going out with. And they definitely want to know what the person loving them looks like! Cupid did not understand that just because the relationship was fine for him, that did not mean it was fine for Psyche.

The second mistake Cupid made was this: after Psyche disobeyed him and saw who he was, he expected that he could leave her and his life would return to what it was before. That is not how love works. When someone becomes a part of your heart and your soul, you are forever changed. There is no going back to who you were before, because who you were does not exist anymore.

That morning when Cupid flew away from Psyche, he knew he was making a big mistake. He wanted to turn around and go back and tell her he was sorry. But he could not do that because he was still more of a child than he was a man. When a man makes a mistake, when a man hurts the woman he loves, he accepts responsibility for hurting her and tells her so. But if that male is still more child than man, he goes off somewhere and pouts. And if he pouts too long, he gets depressed.

That's why Cupid couldn't do anything except lie there

in his bed and stare up at the ceiling, where all he saw was Psyche's face. He would look at it and say, "Why did you have to go and spoil everything? We had a perfect relationship and we would be together now if you had just done what I told you."

But something interesting happened. The more Cupid tried to blame Psyche, the more depressed he got. And that was the best thing that could have happened to him.

I know you must think I'm crazy. Depression is one of the worst feelings there is, but just because you feel bad, it does not mean what is happening to you *is* bad. (And, Jupiter knows: I have been depressed enough to know what I'm talking about.)

Slowly Cupid began to realize he could not spend his life blaming Psyche, and maybe, just maybe, he was the one who had been at fault. The minute he had that thought, he started moving away from being a child and toward becoming an adult.

Cupid's depression broke. Shame washed over him like wave after wave of ocean water striking the beach. He started to cry, but his tears were not because he missed Psyche. His tears were ones of regret over how he had used Psyche for his own gratification. He had never stopped to think about her and what she might have wanted and needed. There would never be a relationship until what she wanted was as important as what he wanted. And he cried aloud.

Far below, in the cold, dark basement, Psyche heard.

The Final Task

Neither Cupid nor Psyche slept well that night. Neither did Venus. The goddess had been unsettled by her last encounter with Psyche. The girl had dared look her directly in the eyes. It was if she were no longer afraid of what Venus might do to her. And no wonder. Whatever Venus sent her to do, she emerged not only unscathed but triumphant. The other gods and goddesses were laughing openly at Venus now whenever she went into the center of Olympus. Even Mars had snickered when she walked past him last evening. Venus would be laughed out of Olympus if she did not come up with a plan to be done with Psyche once and for all.

The goddess lay awake much of the night, thinking and plotting. When she finished, she was amazed at her brilliance. The plan was the most elaborate anyone could have devised, because it was filled with hidden snares. Not only would it be hard for any person or creature to help Psyche, but even if someone did, the final snare, the hidden heart of the plan, could not fail, because it used Psyche's weakness against her.

As soon as Psyche had finished her breakfast of fruit and was brought up from the basement, Venus rushed into the room.

"Good morning," the goddess greeted her pleasantly. "I hope you slept well."

"Thank you, Goddess. I did."

"I'm pleased to hear that, because the task you are to perform today requires that you be well rested."

Psyche noticed that Venus was holding a small box made of inlaid mother-of-pearl.

"Yes," Venus began, noticing Psyche looking at the box. "Isn't it beautiful? Neptune had it made especially for me. I want you to take the box and go to the underworld, to the death palace of the god Pluto, the ruler of the underworld, and his queen, Proserpine. You are to give the box to her and tell her the following: 'The lady Venus sends her compliments and asks that you put into the box a little of your beauty and send it back with the one who brings it. I have been so worried about my son, who is not well, that I have depleted my store of beauty until there is scarcely any left.'

"When Queen Proserpine returns the box to you, you are to come back here immediately. The muses are giving a performance tonight at the Apollo Theater, and I cannot attend looking like an old hag. It's all your fault I look like this. If you had failed at one of the tasks I gave you and died, my life would be back to normal. But since it seems that you are indestructible and simply won't die, I should at least have my beauty back. You're the one who has caused me to lose it, thus you are the one who must help me reclaim it."

Venus handed the box to Psyche, then kissed her lightly on the cheek. "Hurry, child. The performance is tonight and I cannot miss it! And I am certain that Cupid would be delighted to escort you to it." With that, the goddess turned and walked rapidly away.

Psyche's heart rose at Venus's words. Then it fell just as quickly. If she let herself believe anything Venus said, she was a fool. No goddess would give in to the desires of a mortal, and especially no mortal hated as much as Venus did Psyche. Why was Venus sending her to the kingdom of death if she did not want her to remain there? Was it possible for a living person to enter Pluto's realm and return? Didn't one have to be already dead to enter the underworld? And how exactly did someone who was alive enter?

As Psyche left Venus's palace, the little confidence she had received from Jupiter's eagle the day before was waning. Even the deities were loathe to enter Pluto's realm. But maybe she could find someone who could tell her a little about that bleak realm. She did not even know how to get to it.

Psyche went into the center of Olympus, where all the deities and their servants were hurrying to get ready for that evening's festivities. There were lines outside the barbershop and the beauty parlor, the tailor's shop and the cobbler's. "An Evening with the Muses" was the biggest social event of the Olympian year. Everybody who was anybody attended, arrayed in their finest clothes and jewels. And that was why Aeolus, the keeper of the Winds, was there with his wife, Cyane, and the Four Winds: Favonius, Aquilo, Eurus, and Auster.

Though he was a mortal, Aeolus was the inventor of sails

and possessed the gift of predicting the weather, a skill the deities often had need of before they undertook their earthly adventures. Aeolus was a favorite of Jupiter, and each year, the god invited Aeolus, Cyane, and the Four Winds to sit in his box and enjoy the muses's performances.

That is how it came about that Favonius saw Psyche wandering among the crowd, looking around as if she were seeking someone in particular.

"There's Psyche!" West Wind exclaimed.

Aeolus, Cyane, and the Winds stopped to look. They had developed an affection for her from Favonius's description of her beauty and his stories about her and her sisters.

"She looks worried," Cyane said. "Shall we see if she needs help?"

And before Aeolus could respond, Cyane was jumping up and down, waving an arm, and shouting, "Psyche! Psyche! Over here!"

"Don't do that!" Aeolus said firmly to his wife. The Four Winds had told him what had been going on between Venus and Psyche, and he was reluctant to interfere in matters that concerned the deities. "Please, stop! Psyche is none of our business."

As soon as he heard his words, he wanted to take them back. His wife was named for Cyane, a female spirit who had seen Pluto kidnap Proserpine and take her to the underworld.

Cyane was a water nymph. She lived in a pool of water and rose up and tried to stop Pluto when he grabbed

Proserpine. But she was no match for the god of the dead. Cyane was heartbroken at her failure, and she grieved so much that she eventually dissolved into the waters of her pool.

When Ceres came looking for her daughter Proserpine, Cyane could not tell her what she had seen. But Ceres saw Proserpine's girdle floating on the pool of water and had a clue as to her daughter's whereabouts.

Cyane the wife of Aeolus had wondered if she would ever have the opportunity to do something as heroic as her namesake had done. As her eyes met Psyche's and she saw the worry in them, Cyane wondered if this was the day she would become worthy of her name.

She hurried to meet Psyche—Aeolus and the Four Winds following.

"Psyche!" a familiar voice called to her.

Psyche recognized the voice of Favonius and then felt his familiar arms around her. "Oh, I am so happy you are here!" she exclaimed.

After everyone introduced themselves, Psyche told them all that had happened to her and what Venus was demanding of her now.

"Venus is such a bitch!" Cyane exclaimed.

"Shhhh!" Aelous cautioned her.

"Don't you come shushing me!" Cyane told him. "Look at this poor child! What did she do to deserve this?"

"This is none of our business. We should not interfere in the affairs of the gods and goddesses."

"And why not? They interfere in our business anytime they please! Why shouldn't we interfere in theirs every now and then?"

While Aeolus was a cautious man by nature, he was also a man who listened closely and deeply. He had to, because the merest wisp of South Wind could portend an awful storm, and he had to be alert so he could warn people. If he could hear the quietest inhalation of an ill wind, then he certainly could hear his wife, who did not know what a whisper was.

"You're right," he agreed. "The gods are not always just, nor are they always right. And, in this instance, it is obvious that Venus is being ruled by jealousy and not love. But what can we do?"

Aquilo, North Wind, answered immediately. "Well, I've been spending time in the underworld. Pluto has given me some great ideas about how to blow snow in mortals' faces and how to use cold to burn their cheeks and ears, and just so many other things I would never have thought of."

"Didn't I tell you—," Aeolus began before Cyane stopped him.

"Save it! Now is not the time for you and Aquilo to get into one of your arguments."

Reluctantly, Aeolus agreed. "Go on, Aquilo."

"Yes, well, as I was saying. I've been studying with Pluto and I've learned much about how things function in the underworld. I think I know exactly how Psyche can go, then return safely."

"That's wonderful!" they all agreed.

Aquilo turned to Auster, South Wind. "Is not Taenarus in your realm?"

Auster thought for a moment, then brightened. "Yes. It's on a peninsula and is not easy to find. I don't go there often because"—he stopped as he realized what he was about to say—"because there's a hole to the underworld there."

"That's what I thought. Will you take her there?"

"It will be my pleasure. Favonius should not be the only one who gets to have such a beautiful woman in his arms."

Aquilo now turned to Cyane. "I need two pieces of barley bread that have been soaked in honey water."

Cyane looked around until she saw the bakery. "I'll be right back."

"Aeolus, can you give me two coins?" Aquilo asked.

"Of course." He reached in his pocket, took out the coins, and gave them to Aquilo.

When Cyane returned, Aquilo proceeded to tell Psyche everything she must do if she was going to go to the underworld and return.

Psyche repeated everything Aquilo told her, until she had it memorized.

"Good!" Cyane praised her. Then she turned to the others. "Leave us for a moment. I must speak with Psyche, as one woman to another." Cyane put her arm around Psyche's shoulders and hugged her tightly. "I envy you."

Psyche was shocked. "Why would anyone envy me?"

"Because the Fates are putting you to a test to see if you are worthy."

"Worthy of what?"

"Of love. Of the child you are carrying. If you do everything Aquilo has told you, you will return safely. Then if Venus insists on torturing you even more, Aeolus and I will go to Jupiter ourselves and insist that he make her stop."

The two hugged. "Thank you for everything," Psyche said.

"Auster? It's time," Cyane called to South Wind.

Cyane gave Psyche another warm hug. "The end of your troubles will soon be over. After you accomplish this task, I do not see how Venus cannot see that you are worthy to be her daughter-in-law."

"I hope you are right."

Then Aeolus, Auster, Aquilo, Eurus, and Favonius each hugged Psyche.

"Are you ready?" Auster asked.

"I am," Psyche said firmly.

Auster picked her up and Psyche was off to the mouth of the underworld.

The Underworld

Every time I get to this part of the story, it reminds me of all the times I've had to go to the underworld. Everybody who wants to be an adult has got to go to the underworld. The underworld in the story is a physical place. Or is it?

Stories are interesting in that way. Sometimes when a story says a rose is a rose, it is a rose. But then, there are times when the story says a rose, and the rose is not only a rose, it is also something else. When I think about the underworld, I think about the feelings inside myself that I might not want to look at too closely, or even admit that the feelings are a part of me. But going to the underworld also makes me think about the times in my life when I didn't know what I was doing or why I was doing it, but I knew I had to do it. Those are the times like what both Cupid and Psyche are going through right now. Neither one of them can be the person they used to be. But they are not yet the person they are going to be. They don't even know who that person is. Neither Cupid nor Psyche can become new people—and by that I mean adults—until the childish part of themselves dies.

Cupid had been lying in bed like a dead person in a casket. Psyche had been lying in the basement like someone put in a grave. Cupid's "death" was close to an end, but Psyche's was not yet complete. These deaths and underworlds are not the same for men and women. I could try to explain that, but the story is jumping up and down on my foot and pulling on my shirt because it wants to know what is going to happen to Psyche. Isn't that interesting? Even a story doesn't know how it is going to turn out because who knows what a storyteller will say once he or she gets going good. Sometimes even I don't know until I hear the words coming out of my mouth.

Psyche's Journey
to the Underworld

Auster held Psyche close to him. "Hold on tightly," he told her as he flew swiftly above the clouds.

"Why are you flying so fast and so high?" Psyche wanted to know, remembering the slow, leisurely flights she had taken with Favonius.

"If I were to fly this fast below the clouds, I would destroy the dwellings and palaces of mortals. And my brothers and I honor the others' realms and use our destructive powers only within our own realms.

"The other reason I must move swiftly is because we have far to go. Taenarus is at the very edge of the southern realm. Beyond it there is only cold and snow and ice."

Psyche remembered that when she was a child, travelers had come to the palace and told stories about other lands. There was one place in particular where it was always cold and the earth was covered with something one traveler had called snow and ice. Psyche had thought the traveler made up the story to gain favor with her father, who had been known to reward handsomely those whose tales he especially enjoyed.

She wanted to ask Auster if he could fly over this

landscape where neither dirt nor plant existed, but she did not want to get distracted. Aquilo had given her very detailed instructions as to what she should and should not do, what she should and should not say in the underworld. She would better use the time of the flight to go over everything one more time. There was no room for failure. If a mortal entered the realm of the dead and erred in the slightest, he would remain there forever, a living being among the countless shadows, which was all that remained of the dead. And this time she knew that no one would come to rescue her. She was on her own.

Psyche did not know how long they flew, but she noticed when Auster began descending.

"Are we getting close?"

"Yes."

"I can't see anything. It's like we're flying inside a cloud."

"Taenarus is always shrouded in fog," he told her. "It is from the vapors rising from the entrance hole to Pluto's realm. But hold on tight. I'll see what I can do."

Psyche had barely tightened her grip when Auster began turning in wide circles, faster than he had flown before, so fast that Psyche had to close her eyes to keep from getting dizzy.

"There!" he called out.

Psyche opened her eyes. The fog had not dissipated entirely but was much thinner now, and she saw a long piece of land jutting out into a sea as gray as sorrow.

"Is that it?" she shouted to Auster.

"Yes. That is Taenarus."

"Does anyone live there?"

"No one. The land is very rocky. But even if it were not, who would want to live in this place and, day after day, watch the shadows of those who have just died go into the hole with a sadness only the dead can know?"

Coming from a land where the sunlight seemed to dance with the blue waves of the sea, Psyche never imagined that a place so desolate could exist. The ground was covered with stones and boulders, but at the very edge of the peninsula, where its tip extended into the sea, she made out a large hole out of which smoke came steadily in a quiet, thin stream.

"Is-is that the way to the underworld?" she asked, shuddering as she pointed at the hole.

"It is," Auster replied solemnly.

Psyche turned her head away, not wanting to look, but in doing so she saw a procession of people walking along the rocky shore and toward the peninsula. Slowly she realized that these were not people. They were shadows, long and dark like the shadows cast by the sun, except these shadows were upright, shoulders bowed and bodies slumped.

As Auster flew lower, Psyche heard moans coming from the shadows.

"Are those—?"

"The dead," Auster replied, knowing what she was asking.

"Why are they moaning like that?"

"They moan because they are dead."

"But I thought when you were dead it was like being asleep except you could never wake up."

"No. The dead live but without any of the joys of the living. Death is an eternity of sadness."

Psyche blanched as she thought about the times recently when she had wanted to kill herself.

"You must be careful of the shadows. They are waiting for Mercury to take them to the ferry. He does not like this part of his job, but the shadows do tell him all kinds of interesting gossip. And they will seek to entice you with their words. Do not listen. They want nothing more than to persuade you to change places with them. When someone takes his own life, it is because a shadow persuaded him to change places."

Psyche gulped. "I'll not let that happen."

"I hope not, dear Psyche. All the deities are on your side, you know."

"I didn't know. Juno and Ceres did not act like it when I appealed to them for help."

"That does not mean that you do not have their sympathies. You do."

Auster set her down gently a short distance from the hole that led to the underworld.

"Well, here you are," he said. "Remember all that Aquilo told you. If you do, everything will turn out well. You have the two pieces of bread soaked in honey water?"

"Yes."

"And the two coins?"

She pulled them from her pocket.

"Put them in your mouth. That is where Charon will take them from."

Psyche smiled at Auster's concern. "Do not fear. I remember everything I was told. I will be all right."

"Well, then, I will let you go. I will be waiting to return you to Olympus. In fact, all four of us will accompany you in a triumphal return."

"Thank you, Auster."

Psyche felt rather than saw Auster leave. Then she took a deep breath and turned toward the gaping hole from which wispy smoke came. As she made her way slowly over the sharp stones, she realized that she was not afraid, because she knew what was going to happen. She would bring Venus her box of beauty, and then, if the goddess would not relent, Jupiter would make her.

And with that thought, Psyche saw that she had arrived at the hole, and without hesitating, she entered the underworld.

Psyche in the Underworld

Immediately after she stepped through the thick fog shrouding the entrance to the underworld, Psyche found herself on a road as broad and smooth as the one that led from her father's palace into the village. The road went down in a gentle and barely perceptible slope. Though she could not see any torches or lanterns, the way was lighted, not brightly, but more than enough for her to see where she was going.

She walked for some time until, ahead of her, she saw a donkey loaded down with wood and hobbling on three legs. As she came closer, she saw the donkey's owner, a crippled and bald old man in drab and dirty clothes, leaning heavily on a cane. Just as she started to walk past, the load of wood on the donkey's back suddenly fell to the ground.

"Princess! Princess!" called out the man. "Please, help me! As you can see, I am crippled and I cannot pick up all this wood and put it back on the donkey. It won't take much of your time, Princess. Please help an old, crippled man."

Aquilo had warned her about him and the lame donkey, saying, "Do not stop or even speak to the old man." Yet Psyche wanted to. What harm could there be in helping a crippled old man?

"I see you have a kind face, Princess, and a good heart. The gods will reward you if you help me."

The sight of the old man and his piteous voice brought tears to Psyche's eyes. She put her hands over her ears and ran as fast as she could. The crippled man's voice followed her with words of abuse: "I was wrong. You have no heart! May the gods curse you and your children and their children and their children and on to the end of time!"

When Psyche was at a safe distance, she turned and

looked back. The load of wood was no longer strewn across the ground but stacked neatly on the donkey's back, and the old man was now young and standing as straight as the pillars in a temple.

"He almost tricked me into changing places with him," Psyche said to herself softly, amazed at how close she had come to doing exactly what she had been told not to do. "I must be more careful."

She had not walked very far when the road became even wider and she thought she heard something. Psyche stopped and listened. Water. The River of the Dead!

There was a bend in the road, and when Psyche went around it, she saw ahead of her what looked to be hundreds, maybe thousands of shadows walking back and forth along the bank of the river.

"These pathetic shadows were people who were so poor when they died," Aquilo had told her, "they were not buried with a coin beneath their tongues to pay Charon, the ferryman. They are condemned to walk along the banks of the River of the Dead for one hundred years before Charon will take them across."

Hearing Aquilo talk about them was one thing. Seeing them was entirely another. Aquilo could not have prepared her for the continual sounds of their moaning, and their loud cries begging Charon to carry them across. Psyche knew she must get away from the shadows as quickly as she could, or her heart would break with pity.

She walked swiftly and confidently toward the ferry and

Charon. The crowds of shadows on the banks of the river parted as she came toward them, and their moans and pleadings ceased as they gazed at her.

"The goddess of love has come to the underworld!" said one, and quickly the word spread up and down the riverbank that Venus was among them. And the shadows dropped to their knees in adoration.

Psyche ignored them and kept her eyes fixed on Charon standing at the bow of his ferry, a long pole in his hand. He was tall and looked to be as old as the waters he rowed back and forth across. His face was covered with a long, white beard, but she could not make out more of his features because the hood of his long gray cloak was pulled low over his head.

Cyane had warned her to be very careful. Charon had been tricked several times into carrying living mortals across, and Pluto had punished him severely.

"Hercules used his great strength and forced Charon to carry him across," Cyane had said. "Pluto had Charon kept in chains for a year for that mistake. When Orpheus went into the underworld to bring back Eurydice, he charmed Charon by playing beautiful melodies on his lute. Aeneas bribed Charon by giving him a golden bough. Theseus also went to the underworld. No one knew how he had tricked Charon into carrying him over, but Theseus was Theseus. Was there anything he could not do?"

Psyche was not strong like Hercules, nor was she musical like Orpheus, or wise like Theseus, but if Charon had been impressed with Aeneas's golden bough, how could he resist the beauty of which Venus herself was jealous, the beauty that had captured the heart of the god of love?

Charon was known for his ill temper. Who wouldn't be if they did nothing except carry shadows across the River of the Dead from morning until night—and down there, who knew which was which; Charon certainly didn't. Having to listen to the moans and pleas of those without a coin to give him kept Charon in a bad mood. "If they would just shut up for the time it takes the sand to run from the top half of the hourglass to the bottom." Year in, year out, century after century, Charon had to listen to them. If he had not been a god, the sounds of their despair would have driven him mad.

Even worse was the fact that, for millennia now, he had collected a coin from every shadow he rowed across. He was the wealthiest of all the deities, even wealthier than Erebus and Nyx, his parents, who were better known as Darkness and Night. He had so much money that he kept having to add rooms on to his palace so he would have a place to put all the money. But what good was it having more money than anyone who had ever lived if he had no place to spend it! For eons he had begged Pluto to at least let him use some of his money to build a bridge. Shadows could swim across the river, or not. He couldn't care less. But Pluto said it would be ritualistically undignified for shadows to walk across a bridge and into his domain. Undignified! They were dead!

Such was the nature of the silent conversation Charon was having with himself when he saw Psyche approaching the ferry. He knew immediately that she was far from dead. He also knew that he should not take her across: Pluto might put him in chains again. But if a year in chains was the price he had to pay, at least he would have the image of this woman to keep him company.

Psyche's beauty stunned Charon into silence, and when she opened her mouth, he reached in automatically and took the coin from beneath her tongue. He wanted to say something to her, but it had been so long since he had talked to a living mortal. And certainly not to a mortal female. Come to think of it, Charon could not remember the last time he had talked with anyone. There was no point in talking to the dead, because all they would do was moan. He had no idea what to say to Psyche and so he allowed himself to be content with her presence, for which he had no words, anyway.

Psyche could feel Charon's eyes on her like fingers. She did not know if she was more frightened of him or of the River of the Dead, which was unlike any stream she had ever seen. So wide that she could not see the other side, it was dirty brown in color and thick like syrup. It moved slowly and stank like rotting meat.

"Help me!"

Psyche screamed as an arm, the flesh hanging from it in shredded strips, reached up for her from the river.

Charon laughed. "That is a mortal who thought he

could get me to take him across to the underworld." His voice was little more than a scratchy whisper because he had not used it in so long. "He is neither dead nor alive. Unless someone pulls him out, he will spend eternity floating in the gruel of the River of the Dead, calling out for help."

"Help me!" he cried out again, his face rising out of the river.

As ghastly as he was, Psyche knew she would have reached out to him had not Aquilo warned her not to. To protect herself from her own pity she closed her eyes and put her hands over her ears and kept them there until, at long last, she felt the boat touch the other side.

"May the gods be with you," Charon said to Psyche as she left the ferry.

"And you," she replied.

Psyche found herself back on a road like the one that had brought her to the river. She walked quickly now, wanting to get her task over with as soon as possible. She was not sure just how much more of this dismal realm she could endure.

Psyche had not gone far when she came upon three women sitting at looms, weaving. The women were only a little older than she was, and Psyche was so happy to see someone near her age that she began to smile. The cloth they were weaving was deep red in color and threaded at regular intervals with strips of orange. It reminded her of daylight, sunshine, warmth, and happiness, everything this realm was not. How had three such lovely young women come to be here?

Psyche wanted a closer look at what they were weaving and was about to go over to them when she remembered: "After you get off Charon's ferry, you will encounter three women weaving. Do not take pity on them. They are there only to try to take from you the two pieces of bread you are carrying. Please understand, dear Psyche. If you lose even one piece of bread, you will not be able to return to this world."

Reluctantly, Psyche walked by and continued on her way.

The road was more narrow now and going down, deeper and deeper, into the underworld. As eager as Psyche was to fulfill her task and leave, her steps slowed as she came closer to her destination and the darkness deepened until it shone with the luster of jewels.

Suddenly, Psyche stopped. She thought she heard something. She listened. Yes, there it was again! It sounded like all the animals on the face of the earth had come together in one place and were engaged in a fight to the death. But Psyche knew what it was—Cerberus, the guardian of the gates to Pluto's palace, the place Proserpine lived for half of each year.

Though she knew what she was supposed to do to get safely by Cerberus, she was not sure she could. The sounds made by the beast were so ferocious, she feared that the noise alone would devour her. She knew that was not true, but sometimes truth is not as fierce as fear. How could a morsel of bread distract such a creature? She did not know. She had no choice but to have faith in what Aquilo had told her.

Psyche moved forward very slowly, the noise getting louder and louder as she came closer and closer. She could see him now, standing before the gates to Pluto's palace. He had three heads of dogs and the long tail of a dragon, and along his back grew the heads of snakes. Each dog's head looked in a different direction and snarled and snapped, saliva dripping from their teeth and tongues.

Psyche did not look directly into the eyes of the head pointed in her direction, but reached in her pocket for one of the pieces of bread. She threw it a good distance to the side and away from the gate. The head that was watching it immediately went in the direction of the bread and the rest of the beast had no choice but to follow.

Quickly Psyche went through the gate and closed it behind her. She found herself in a large field with a path through the center. However, the field was not covered with grass and flowers like every other field she had ever seen. This one was thick with plants, all of different shades of green, and most amazing of all, the plants seemed to be speaking, because Psyche heard the low murmur of talk.

As she started down the path, she heard the plants more distinctly as she passed them:

"I am baneberry. Taste my leaves."

"I am belladonna. Taste my leaves."

"I am bloodroot. Taste my leaves."

But there was something in the way the plants introduced themselves that made Psyche suspicious. When she passed a plant that introduced itself as Death Angel Mushroom, she remembered. Her father liked to walk in the woods, and when she was young he would take her on walks and point out plants she should not even touch. One, she recalled, was Death Angel Mushroom. Were all these plants poisonous?

As if in response, the entire field of plants erupted into cackling laughter and then began shouting their names:

"Hemlock!"

"Mandrake!"

"Moonseed!"

"Wolfsbane!"

Psyche covered her ears and ran until she was out of the field. The path continued into a forest of tall trees, but trees unlike any she had ever seen. They were a pale, ghostly white with bloodred twisted limbs and branches. She wondered if the trees were going to introduce themselves, but as she continued along the path among them, there was only silence.

Finally, she emerged from the forest to find herself standing before a palace built from thick slabs of darkness. Psyche knew if she stood there looking at the building, she would become too frightened to go inside, so she hurried toward what looked to be the doorway. But there was no door handle, though this had to be the door, because it was set in from the rest of the building. How was she supposed to get inside?

Maybe the door was already unlocked and all she had to do was push it. She did so, and she gave a little scream when her hands, instead of meeting something solid, went through the blackness. Psyche pulled her hands back and looked at them. They looked the same. She rubbed one hand with the other. They felt the same, so she put her hands out again. Very carefully, she pushed against the darkness. Her hands went through. She followed her hands and arms and found herself on the other side of the darkness and in a large room, larger even than the Great Hall in her father's palace.

There, at the far end of the large room, sat a woman on a throne of bleached bones. She was pale and looked as if all the blood had been drained from her body, yet there was no mistaking her beauty. Her dark hair was parted in the middle and so long that it almost touched the floor beneath her throne. As Psyche came closer, she could see a smile on Proserpine's thin lips.

"Greetings," the Queen of Death said.

Psyche curtsied. "My lady."

"What a delight to see a living person, and one of such extraordinary beauty. Living here as I do for half of each year, there are times when I miss the world above. You must sit and stay awhile. I will order my servants to bring you food and drink so that you might relax and renew yourself."

How Psyche wished she could have time to relax and eat something delicious. But Aquilo had warned her against accepting Proserpine's invitation.

"Your invitation is very gracious," Psyche responded, as she sat down on the floor. "I wish I had the time to avail myself of your hospitality but I do not. However, if I could have just a piece of bread, it would be more than sufficient to raise my spirits."

"As you wish," Proserpine answered, and a servant appeared out of the air and offered Psyche a piece of bread on a plate made from bone.

"Since a mortal risks his soul by coming here while still alive, you must have urgent business. What can I do for you?"

"Not for me, but for the goddess Venus."

"I would be more than happy to do anything Venus would ask of me."

Psyche produced the mother-of-pearl box. "The goddess has been under a great deal of stress of late, and her supply of beauty is running low. She asks that you fill this box with some of your beauty. She doesn't need much. Enough for a day."

"It will be a pleasure."

Proserpine took the box from Psyche, went behind the throne, and disappeared. Before long she reappeared and handed the box to Psyche.

"There. Please give this to Venus and tell her that I look forward to seeing her soon. It is almost time for me to bring spring back to the northern places of the world above."

Psyche stood up. "Thank you, my lady."

She curtsied and then hurried away. "I did it! I did it!" Psyche whispered over and over to herself. She couldn't believe it. By herself, without any help from ants, Pan, or a giant bird, she had come to the heart of the underworld and spoken to the Queen of Death.

So elated was she that she ran through the forest of ghost-white trees, through the field of poisonous plants, and slowed only when she came to the gate guarded by Cerberus. She reached in her pocket and took her last piece of bread and threw it a distance from the gate. The three-headed dog ran to get it, and Psyche hurried through the gate, past the three women weaving, and up the slope to the River of the Dead.

Charon stood with his ferry, as if waiting for her. Psyche put the remaining coin in her mouth, then got on the ferry and opened her mouth. Charon took the coin.

Once the ferry reached the other side, Psyche began running again, clutching the box close to her breasts. She passed the lame man and his lame donkey and the fallen pile of wood, and before she knew it, she could see the entrance of the hole.

"I did it! I did it!" she shouted aloud now as she burst through the hole and into the gray light of Taenarus. She hurried over the stony earth until she came to a field, and there, she lay down and flung her arms out.

"I did it!" she screamed as loud as she could. "I did it!" And she laughed and laughed and laughed.

She lay there for a while to catch her breath and to let the enormity of what she had accomplished sink in. Finally, she sat up, feeling rested, and began searching the skies for Auster, who said he would know when she had emerged from Pluto's realm.

Psyche still found it hard to believe that her ordeal was finally at an end and she was, at long last, going to see Cupid. Then she realized, with horror, "I probably look worse than a kitchen maid." She did not have a mirror but she was sure she looked frightful. She ran her fingers through her hair and it was a tangled mess. Her gown was dirty and torn in places. And her face! She did not want to try to imagine how it must look after all she had been through.

Psyche looked at the box she was carrying. She could hear Aquilo's voice telling her not to open the box. But what harm could it do if she took a little of the beauty Proserpine had put inside? She didn't need much. Just enough to make her look as beautiful as Cupid remembered. She had done everything Aquilo had told her to do. Neither he nor Venus would know she opened the box.

Psyche lifted the cover slowly. Out came a large cloud of black smoke. Startled, she screamed, but the smoke enveloped her and choked off her cry.

Psyche slumped to the ground—as if she were dead.

Cupid's Decision

While Psyche was making her way into and out of the underworld, events were unfolding at Venus's palace.

Every evening Venus went to see Cupid. All she wanted was for him to apologize for the pain he had inflicted on her. Venus did not think that was too much to expect after he had so blatantly disobeyed her and made her a mockery among the deities.

Perhaps Cupid would have given his mother the apology she felt she needed if she had not been so insistent about it. But day after day he lay in bed, his body turned away from her, and listened as she paced back and forth across the room, ranting and pleading. What he heard startled him.

Venus's words were not about him; they were only about herself. Nothing mattered except her hurt at his disobedience, her disappointment that he had not lived up to her expectation, and the embarrassment he had caused her.

But what had he done that was so awful? Why was he on the receiving end of so much anger and wrath? All he had done was fall in love, which was not something he had planned or sought.

Love happened. Love came to show you that you could be more than you could ever imagine, because love forced you out of the narrows of yourself and thrust you into a vastness that stretched from one end of time to the other.

Nothing mattered except being in the presence of love, the greatest beauty of all.

But he had foolishly thrust Psyche away. Why? Because she had disobeyed him. With sadness he realized that he had acted toward Psyche as Venus was acting toward him. He sought to punish Psyche for disobeying him, just as Venus punished him for disobeying her.

Venus was angry because she had lost control of her relationship with him. How was that different from his anger at Psyche for looking at him? It wasn't. He had not known how much he was like his mother.

That evening when Venus unlocked the door and entered his chambers, she was surprised to see him standing at the far end of the room. She smiled. "Has he finally come to his senses?" she wondered. Was he now going to apologize for how much he had hurt her?

When Cupid heard the door open, he turned to face his mother.

"I have a question for you," he said before she could utter a word.

"Of course, dear."

Cupid walked across the room and stood before her. Venus had never seen such intensity in his eyes. She wasn't sure she liked what she was seeing.

"Why are you so angry?" he asked.

Venus was flustered. "I-I-I'm not angry, dear. I'm hurt."

"Why?"

"Because you disobeyed me. You allowed yourself to become bewitched by my enemy, someone whose beauty threatens to usurp my place in the hearts of mortals."

Cupid laughed softly. "And that's what I don't understand. Since you knew how beautiful she was, why did you send me to her? If you were so afraid of her beauty, why didn't you do everything in your power to make sure I never saw her?"

Venus opened her mouth to speak, then slowly closed it. There was nothing to say. Could it be that she had desired what she claimed she hated? Why had she been so sure Cupid would be immune to Psyche's beauty when she herself had seen that beauty as a threat? She had no answer.

"I must find her. Where is she, Mother? Is she here? What have you done to her?"

Venus turned to walk away, but Cupid grabbed her by the arm and turned her around. "Where is Psyche, Mother?"

"You're hurting me," Venus complained at the tightness of Cupid's grip on her arm.

"And you are hurting me. Where is Psyche?"

Venus looked up at Cupid, tears in her eyes. "Why are you doing this to me?"

"This is not about you. I know you find that hard to believe. But this has nothing to do with you. This is about me."

"But she's a mortal!"

"Like Adonis?"

Venus gasped.

"Is that why you do not want me to love Psyche? You lost Adonis, and now, you do not want me to have happiness."

Venus dropped her head in shame. Was she so selfish that she would deny love to her son because love had been taken from her?

"I sent Psyche to the underworld," she said quietly, her head still down.

"You *what*?" Cupid exclaimed.

"I sent her to the underworld to get a box of beauty from Proserpine. But . . . but I told Proserpine not to put beauty in the box." Venus stopped.

"What did you tell her to put in it?" Cupid demanded to know.

"I told her to fill it with a cloud of death. I told Psyche not to open the box, but I doubt there exists a woman who would not want to take for herself some of what she believes to be divine beauty. When she opens the box, she will be enveloped by a cloud of death."

"Which portal to the underworld did she enter?"

"The one on Taenarus."

Cupid fled—out the door, out of the mansion—and, spreading his wings, flew into the air. He did not know how much time he had, but he knew he had to hurry.

As he left Olympus and entered Earth's sky, Favonius saw him.

"Cupid!"

"Favonius! I need your help. Psyche is in danger and I

am afraid I cannot fly fast enough to reach her in time. Will you help me?"

"We all will!" The western wind sent strong currents to the east, north, and south to summon his brothers. Never had all four of them used their powers at the same time, but Favonius knew no other way to get Cupid to Taenarus in time to save Psyche. Favonius did not know if the world could withstand the power of all four winds blowing at the same time, but nothing mattered now except Psyche's life.

The Four Winds went as high into the sky as they could to lessen the effect on Earth. They merged into one great force, and holding on to Cupid, they blew across the heavens. They moved with such power and speed that they tore the blue out of the sky. When Sun saw what was happening, he took blues from all those he collected at the end of each day and hurriedly restored the sky to its rightful color.

Cupid was glad the Four Winds were holding him as tightly as they were. Otherwise he would have been blown clear out of the universe. But in the space between the beat of his heart, Cupid was set down at Taenarus just as the cloud of death billowed out of the box and enveloped Psyche.

Without hesitating Cupid rushed to the cloud. Careful not to enter it himself, he used his wings to push the cloud back into the box. However, a thin layer of the cloud covered Psyche like a veil. Slowly, carefully, Cupid brushed it off and into the box.

Then he kissed Psyche softly on the lips. Her eyes fluttered open and when she saw Cupid's face above hers, she put her arms around his neck and the two held each other as if they would never again let go.

After the Four Winds had disentangled themselves from each other, they picked up Cupid and Psyche. Slowly and majestically, they carried the two across the heavens and through to the other side, where all Olympus waited, the gods and goddesses having witnessed for themselves Cupid's rescue of Psyche from death.

The deities walked in procession behind the two lovers as they made their way to Jupiter's palace, where he waited with Apollo and Venus.

"Welcome!" Jupiter greeted them. "It is a good thing this has happened," he addressed the assembled deities. "We all know of what mischief our Cupid is capable. Indeed, even I have not been exempt from the power of his arrows. Now that he knows for himself what it is to love and to lose that love, perhaps he will use his arrows with more consideration."

Cupid blushed and bowed his head. "Indeed, I will."

"Good! We are all relieved to hear that." Then Jupiter turned to Venus. "You, in your wrath, have disappointed me."

"I am sorry," Venus said softly, her head bowed. "Having loved a mortal and lost him to death, I would ask that my son be spared the same eternal anguish."

"So be it. Bring me the nectar of immortality!"

Mercury appeared with a crystal goblet filled with a shining red liquid.

"Come and drink!" Jupiter said to Psyche.

Psyche drank the nectar. Never had she tasted anything so delicately sweet. Her being glowed with warmth as the drink coursed through her body.

"From this day forward, you are immortal," Jupiter told her. "You and Cupid will have eternity for your love. And now, to the feast prepared in your honors!"

Everyone hurried into the Great Hall of Jupiter's palace and sat at the long table filled with dishes of food. But being deities, they did not eat what mortals ate. They dined on salad of pine breath with starshine dressing, ray-of-sunset soup, filet of dawn in a sauce made from the smells of spring, and for dessert, winter custard with cloudberries. Bacchus saw to it that everyone's glasses were always filled with his latest wine made from the flavors of summer.

Then it was time for the formal wedding of Cupid and Psyche. The muses read poetry and played instruments and sang. Apollo played on the lyre a composition of his own making.

Then Jupiter stood before Cupid and Psyche. "I now pronounce you to be married, body to body, and soul to soul, forever and ever."

Cupid took Psyche, not to his palace hidden in the mountains, but to the palace of her mother and father, so she would not be alone during the times he went out to create love among mortals.

Eight months after they were wed, Psyche gave birth to their daughter, whom they named Pleasure.

And so it is when Love and Soul become one.

So it is.

A Final Word

And that's the story of Cupid and Psyche. Of course, if you were listening closely, and I know you were, I bet you heard a lot of your own story, didn't you? That's the tricky thing about stories. You think you're hearing a story about somebody else, and then something clicks and you start to feel that the story is about you.

The interesting thing about this particular story is that it taught me that sometimes I act like Cupid and sometimes I act like Psyche. Stories don't much care who's male and who's female, because everybody has a little of both inside them.

That's why this story and my story and your story, well, they're all the same story. You know what I mean? If this story which was first told way back in the year one hundred fits you and me today like it was ours to begin with, then just because we have different names and different faces, it doesn't mean we're not living the same story. Because we are.

We certainly are.

Author's Note

The story of Cupid and Psyche is found in a book called *The Transformation of Lucius Apuleius of Madaura*, a book we know today as *The Golden Ass*.

Lucius Apuleius lived between 123 and 180 CE. Born in what is now Algeria as the son of a wealthy provincial magistrate, Apuleius was educated in Carthage, Greece, and Rome. He married Pudentila, a wealthy woman, but was accused by her family of using magic to seduce her. In 158, Apuleius was put on trial, defended himself, and was acquitted.

The Golden Ass is the only novel in Latin to have survived antiquity. The most famous story in it is "Cupid and Psyche," which is one of the enduring tales of Western civilization. It is a story I first encountered through my interest in the psychology of Carl Jung. In Jungian psychology the tale is considered an important metaphorical delineation of the archetypal psychology of women. (See Robert Johnson's *She: Understanding Feminine Psychology* and Marie-Luise von Franz's *Golden Ass of Apuleius: The Liberation of the Feminine in Man.*)

My original idea for retelling the story of Cupid and Psyche was to do a book of seventy-five or so pages in which I would basically retell the story, but in the voice of a Southern black storyteller. However, as so often happens, when I started writing, I found myself bothered by what I considered to be gaps in the story, especially the large one in which Cupid simply vanishes from most of the story only to miraculously reappear to save Psyche. So I began researching Greek and Roman mythology and found all kinds of wonderful lesser deities, like Oizys the goddess of pain, Favonius the West Wind, Aeolus the keeper of the winds, and others. Because it was not my intent to faithfully retell Aupelius's story, I have taken deities and figures from both Greek and Roman mythology. I have also brought together all the stories about Cupid (or Eros).

What began as a projected seventy-five-page book became what you have here. I had much fun researching and writing this book, as it became a book I wished I had had during the frightening and difficult years of my own adolescence when I first encountered the mysteries of girls, love, and myself.

The experience of love is the most central and profound of our lives. Yet we are given no instruction in the ways of love. Popular music and movies are our primary sources for what we think love is and should be, and as entertaining as these media are, the views of love they present are more often expressions of sentimentality instead of representations of the very hard realities of what it means to be human and what the act of loving presents us with.

I ended up writing a book in which I shared something of what I've learned over these seven decades through marriages and many wonderful love affairs. Which is not to say that everything the narrator says is autobiographical. The narrator's voice is mine, and then again, it isn't. Some of the opinions he expresses are mine, and some are very definitely his.

I am deeply grateful to Michael Joseph, the moderator of the Child_Lit Internet group of critical theory in children's literature. Michael is a librarian at Rutgers University. As a visiting instructor there, he has taught the tale of Cupid and Psyche—and he knows it and the critical literature surrounding it far better than I. The e-mail conversations we shared were extremely helpful, and he was gracious enough to agree to read the manuscript. His careful reading and insights were invaluable.

I also want to thank Betsy Hearne, professor of library and information services at the University of Illinois, for helping me think through an important element of the story. I came across a reference (I don't recall where now) that said in some versions of the Cupid and Psyche story, the smoke from the box she receives from Proserpine turns her black. I toyed with the idea of making this part of my retelling. Though neither Betsy nor Michael expressed an opinion on my doing this, after exchanging e-mails with them, I decided that doing so would change the focus of the story. But I am still tantalized by the notion of the god of love marrying a black Psyche.

Finally, and as always, I am grateful to the one with

whom I have shared so much love for a decade and a half now, my wife, Milan Sabatini. Since 1991 she has been the first person to read my manuscripts, and all of them, including this one, have been improved enormously by her attention to details.

Julius Lester
Belchertown, Massachusetts
August 30, 2005

Works Consulted

Books

Apuleius. *The Marriage of Cupid and Psyche.* Translated by Walter Paler. New York: Heritage Press, 1951.

———. *The Transformations of Lucius; Otherwise Known as The Golden Ass.* Translated by Robert Graves. New York: Farrar, Straus and Young, 1951.

Birberick, Anne L. *Reading Undercover: Audience and Authority in Jean de la Fontaine.* Lewisburg, Pa.: Bucknell University Press, 1998.

Cavicchioli, Sonia. *The Tale of Cupid and Psyche: An Illustrated History.* New York: George Braziller, 2002.

Craft, Charlotte M. *Cupid and Psyche.* New York: HarperCollins, 1996.

Edwards, Lee R. *Psyche as Hero: Female Heroism and Fictional Form.* Middletown, Conn.: Wesleyan University Press, 1984.

Eliot, Alexander, ed. *Myths.* New York: McGraw-Hill, 1976.

Encyclopedia of World Mythology. Foreword by Rex Warner. New York: Galahad Books, 1975.

Ficino, Marsilio. *Commentary on Plato's Symposium.* Translated by Sears Reynolds Jayne. Columbia, Mo.: University of Missouri Studies, vol. XIX, no. 1, 1944.

Guirand, Félix, ed. *New Larousse Encyclopedia of Mythology.* Translated by Richard Aldington and Delano Ames. New York: Prometheus Press, 1974.

Grant, Michael, and John Hazel. *Who's Who in Classical Mythology.* New York: Oxford University Press, 1993.

Graves, Robert, trans. *The Greek Myths.* New York: George Braziller, Inc., 1957.

Hamilton, Edith. *Mythology.* New York: Little, Brown and Company, 1942.

Hearne, Betsy Gould. *Beauty and the Beast: Visions and Revisions of an Old Tale.* Chicago, Ill.: The University of Chicago Press, 1989.

Herzberg, Max J. *Myths and Their Meaning.* Boston, Mass.: Allyn and Bacon, 1962.

Ovid. *The Metamorphoses of Ovid.* Translated by David Mandelbaum. New York: Harcourt, Brace and Company, 1993.

Walker, Barbara G. *The Woman's Encyclopedia of Myths and Secrets.* New York: Harper & Row, 1983.

Warner, Marina. *From the Beast to the Blonde: On Fairy Tales and Their Tellers.* New York: Farrar, Straus and Giroux, 1995.

Articles

Armstrong, Jennifer. "The Writer's Page: Greeting Beauty." *The Horn Book* (January/February 2005) 81, no. 1: 57–9.

Ross, Lena B. " 'Cupid and Psyche': Birth of a New Consciousness." *Psyche's Stories: Modern Jungian Interpretations of Fairy Tales,* vol. 1. Edited by Murray Stein and Lionel Corbett. Wilmette, Ill.: Chiron Publications, 1991.

Internet Resources

Encyclopedia Mythica: http://www.pantheon.org/
Forum Romanum: http://www.forumromanum.org/
Greek Mythology Link: http://homepage.mac.com/cparada/GML/